SHORT STORIES BY ANDREI CODRESCU

Monsieur Teste in America

& OTHER INSTANCES OF REALISM

COFFEE HOUSE PRESS :: MINNEAPOLIS :: 1987

The author thanks the editors of the following publications in which some of these works first appeared in earlier versions: *Paris Review* for publishing "Monsieur Teste in America" and "Samba de los Agentes;" *New Directions Annual* for publishing "The Herald;" *Departures* for publishing "The Old Couple;" *The Painted Bride Quarterly* for publishing "Julie;" and *Hot Water Review* for publishing "A Bar in Brooklyn." "Samba de los Agentes" also won The Pushcart Prize and was published in PUSHCART VIII (Pushcart Press), and in the Avon paperback edition of the same anthology.

The publishers wish to thank the National Endowment for the Arts for a Small Press Assistance Grant which aided in the publication of this book.

Coffee House Press books are available to bookstores through our primary distributor: Consortium Book Sales and Distribution, 213 East Fourth Street, Saint Paul, Minnesota 55101. Our books are also available through all major library distributors and jobbers, and through most small press distributors, including Bookpeople, Bookslinger, Inland, Pacific Pipeline, and Small Press Distribution. For personal orders, catalogs or other information, write to: Coffee House Press, Post Office Box 10870, Minneapolis, Minnesota 55458.

LIBRARY OF CONGRESS CATALOGING IN PUBLICATION DATA

Codrescu, Andrei, 1946-
  Monsieur Teste in America & other instances of realism.

  1. United States—Social life and customs—
1971-   —Anecdotes, facetiae, satire, etc. I. Title.
II. Title: Monsieur Teste in America and other instances
of realism.
E169.04.C63 1987   973.92   87-27731
ISBN 0-918273-32-3 (pbk. : alk. paper)

CONTENTS

Monsieur Teste in America
AN ARRIVAL AND THE NECESSITY OF IT

AT TWENTY-NINE YEARS OF AGE, completely satisfied with the gentle fall outside, with vast stretches of contentment ahead of me in an unbroken mellow yellow greenery, I took my head in my hands and I considered my position. I WAS BORED IN HEAVEN!

At first, unbelieving, I tried to go on with my daily routines; just at the moment when they could have secured my nights, they got blasted by this realization. "Oh, daily routines," I cried at them as they filled with void, "please do not abandon me! I am only trying to conquer my ambitions, to set my greed to rest in the cool shade of its immediate demands, to give my need for worship a little rest and nostalgia (R & G), to lure the beast of my lust back into the zoo where it belongs, to silence my mind to the point where stupidity *will* be my strong point, to shut up in general, and to shrink physically in particular." Unresponsive to my passionate plea, the daily routines began disintegrating.

With this crisis pending and with the rains not far off,

I opened the part of my brain containing the past and let
it spill in great globular formations across my closed eyes.
My past, tied in neat bundles, each bundle with its own
conclusion written in red ink on the face of it, obeyed me
gently like a river when the Pacific Gas & Electric plant
moves away. Or closes shop.

Who was I? Was I bored in Heaven because I was not
I? Or was I bored because Heaven wasn't I? Was I
boredom or was I Heaven? Was I in Heaven for being I on
Earth? Or was I to be on Earth as the conclusion of
Heaven? It was hard to decide.

When I came to America, to Norte America, I needed
someone to counsel me in the simple secrets. I did not
know such a person. Older exiles who, as myself, had
come here without speaking a word of English, guarded
their simple secrets carefully because their vampiric ambitions depended on them. A man might have three simple
secrets by the age of forty-five if he emigrated at the age of
twenty. A sixty-year-old man who emigrated at fifteen
might have six simple secrets. I didn't have any and no one
gave me theirs. I had to go at it alone, something I have
a horror of. I don't even like going to the bathroom alone.

O Lord! I cannot imagine living without simple secrets!

Well, it took me three years to learn it (a history of
academic excellence) but I did. Here it is:

AMERICA IS EXACTLY THE WAY IT SEEMS TO BE. THERE ARE
NO HIDDEN INTENTIONS.

To a European, this is inconceivable. The whole idea
denies the fundamentals of experience. It is like listening to
a dog laugh. Notice the old Hungarian lady waiting for the
bus. She does not wait for the bus in the square clearly
marked BUS STOP. She runs ahead of the bus before it has
even stopped. The black bus driver shoos her away
furiously. She goes back to the allotted area for boarding
(she still does not believe it!), gets on the bus and starts a
long harangue about the driver's rudeness. "I know my
place," she says, "you should know yours!" As you can

see, she is speaking about human places. Hers & His. Nowhere does it occur to her that there is *a place for boarding.* She does not believe that objects mean what they say. Her definition of objects is *that which is put in front of a woman to mislead her.* If you ask her who put the object there she will laugh. Other people, of course. The hidden intentions of the sign BUS STOP are as clear to her as his watch is to the driver. BUS STOP in her country does not mean BUS STOP. It means also: *crowds, place, age, a public appearance, social position, a lady, engagements.*

Take this same lady and say "chocolate" to her. She will immediately have a vision of rare pleasure. Take the nearest American and say "chocolate" to her. It will mean only *a trip to the drugstore.*

On the other hand, if you seriously pull this lady aside and say "Jim" to her or "Elma" or "Gertrude," she will naturally ask the real questions: is he/she married yet? Do they have children? What are the latest scandals? It would never occur to her to impute an area of shadowy intentions to a person. Objects are the only guilty party. People are blameless to the extent that, although they put the objects there, they understand that it's only a game.

So, the first simple secret that it took me three years to learn was, as I have said, this:

AMERICA CAN BE TAKEN FOR GRANTED. THE OBVIOUS IS VERY SERIOUS ABOUT ITSELF HERE.

In Europe, I knew, the obvious did not exist. It had been riddled with holes there. An intelligent person is supposed to look through these holes before taking a step. And in Europe everybody is intelligent. Except the peasants, of course. But then they are objects anyway.

This one simple secret seemed to me so precious that for the next six years or so I did nothing but bathe in the sunny obviousness of America. (I made quite a bit of money, too.)

Then I became suspicious again. Here was I, twenty-one years old. If America is so obvious, I thought, how does

she do it? A fatal question, friends, and I only hope for
your sake that you are all Americans and never have to ask
that. I looked at the ads for edification. I turned on the
television. My living room floor was littered with
newspapers. I took apart the house appliances. Then I
didn't look at ads, TV, newspapers or appliance innards
any longer and I instantly forgot what I saw in the ads,
TV, newspapers and appliances. And thus, with the swift-
ness of electroshock, I comprehended a *second* simple
secret:

DON'T LOOK BACK! THEY MIGHT BE GAINING ON YOU!

This is when I began my long affair with the American
language. If everything were obvious and firmly pro-
gressive it meant, naturally, that the language was a virgin
expanse of snow on which my footsteps, if firm enough,
could lead the rescuing party to me. So you see the psychological basis on which this affair thrived: I planned to use,
yes, use the innocence of the language to further my aims
which were neither more nor less than cracking the safe
holding all the simple secrets of America. (Think of all the
money I was going to make!)

O what a language! Contagious words imbued with
mass-market meanings like a sponge full of ink crowded
my mind to dictate their grammar to me! This grammar I
was, of course, cautious to disregard as any lover would
disregard his beloved's family if they didn't approve.
Grammar did not approve of me so I didn't approve of
grammar, and I continued in spite of its protestations to
love the language to distraction. With one move I would
suck the structural juice of grammar and spit it on the
ground while with another move I would gather brilliant
clusters of adjectives to my bosom and caress them into action. I discovered, o tender passion, that one is never alone
with words in America. Vast masses of people accom-
panied each word to its place in the dictionary. These
masses did what I did, ate what I ate, thought what I
thought. The words of America's language brought me an

incalculable dowry. They put at my disposal all the natives of the Norte America continent to dispose of as I saw fit. I was not anxious to hide from these folks even though I could never be intimate with my beloved. I despise intimacy and the bourgeois heart of it. I loved to sit still, surrounded by words truly open like transparent glass buildings without any doors in and out of which thousands of people jumped into their obvious business.

"If I could just have your words forever, my tongue," I whispered, "to fit them to my good intentions like silencers to guns, I could, conceivably, own the continent."

Above my bed, during this affair (we rarely left the bed, my darling and I) stood this injunction by Bill Knott:

PEOPLE WHO GET DOWN ON THEIR KNEES TO ME ARE THE ANSWERS TO MY PRAYERS

But, alas, no human passion is made to last. Like eggs, passions must be stuck in a refrigerator of the spirit, and this I was not willing to do.

At the age of twenty-four, I began to lose my enchantment. (And I wasn't making any money. A good agency of the government [welfare] understood my plight and saw to it that I sat in bed but it didn't pay much.)

Also, around this time, a tremendous nostalgia began to quake in me. I could barely remember my native tongue and I missed the fabulous capacity for abstraction that I had had before coming to America.

In this depressed state I moved into the wilderness, resolving to never speak, want or ask for anything. The wilderness had served this purpose until today when, looking at the purple and gold noose in the clouds above the ocean, I realized this horror: I AM BORED IN HEAVEN!

There was someone I knew who had the cure to my ills. It was the mentor of my youth, the man most responsible for setting the tender bones of my mind in the position in which they are now, the man who inspired me with his shining example, the man to whom I owed my ability to think: Monsieur Teste.

Summoning the remains of my strength, I dragged myself to the tiny post office of the nearest forgotten community (a nouveau old town inhabited by the nouveau poor) and I dictated the following telegram to the startled postmistress whose siesta had never until then been interrupted:

> MONSIEUR TESTE stop PLEASE COME TO stop AS stop YOU ALWAYS stop HAD stop PARIS stop EUROPE stop

Two days later, the postmistress, terrified, unable to control her gothic features from glowing in the moonlight, appeared at the window of my modest treehouse and handed me the following:

> ARRIVING stop IN NEW YORK stop BY BOAT stop APRIL 13 1974 stop MONSIEUR TESTE stop

I was twenty-nine years old that day.

*

NEW YORK with its usual disagreeable sense of humor lay under the general strike like an actress under a Foreign Legionnaire.

It was an ominous sign and downright depressing when I realized that Monsieur Teste had arrived but could not get off the boat because nobody would lower the gangplanks. There I sat, straining my eyes past the Statue of Liberty, trying to catch a glimpse of my savior among the black dots the fog jotted around the liner CALYPSO. The America Monsieur Teste was going to step on at the end of the strike was not the America I had found at my arrival. In my time, in 1966, America was a cluster of bubbles fighting to boil its human stew in a combination of exotic spices: Buddhism, mysticism, Marxism, etc. Now, in 1974, the ground was solid, the stew had been eaten and the people of America lay on their backs digesting quietly while murmuring, in unison: DOWN WITH ECCENTRICITY! BACK TO REALISM! Only realism did not upset the stomach. God was not in fashion any more. Survival was.

I was curious to see how Monsieur Teste would take it. He was not used to politeness. And originality was on the wane.

When I finally had the chance to say "Welcome, Monsieur Teste," three days later, and hand him the bag of grapefruit I thought would stand for flowers, my curiosity had reached its boiling point.

He walked slowly across the deck, tall, skinny, grim-faced, dressed in a three-piece suit with an artificial zinnia in the lapel. Although he was walking in my direction, he looked insistently to his left side as if he had dropped his watch in the water. When he came close, he lifted a pale blue set of eyes, planted them into my own brown ones, and took the bag of grapefruits out of my hand without a word. I took his suitcase, which was very light (Monsieur Teste travelled, as he had always, with only a toothbrush, an aluminum canteen filled with mineral water and a complicated mathematical instrument laid carefully at the bottom of a small velvet-lined case) and he took my hand, which was very sweaty (since my earliest childhood) and thus, hand in hand, we put our four feet at once down on the New Land. I had the curious feeling that I too was arriving to America for the first time. Everything looked unfamiliar. It's Teste's immediate influence, I thought. Without a word he had already began teaching me my old ways.

"Well, what do you think?" I said, including, with a sweeping gesture, the tall towers of Manhattan, the deserts of Nevada, my treehouse in California, my efforts at understanding and my present bafflement.

He didn't answer. He didn't make a gesture, either, because he had, as I knew, killed his puppet as far back as 1923. I would have given my kingdom just then for a clenching of his fist.

Later, sitting in one of those "luncheonettes" for which New York is justly famous, I ordered two bowls of blood red cabbage borscht for Teste and myself. In silence, with a collective mouth, we set ourselves upon the blood red

liquid and shlurped intimately at each other like waves lap-
ping on a beach. We were off to a good start. Monsieur
Teste rose.

"The unknown makes me shit well," he said, by way of
his first words in Norte America.

While he did his business in there I let contentment
spread through my bones which together with the warmth
generated by the borscht squeaked in utter delight. My
bones! It was the first time since coming to this country
that I had thought of my bones. Like a loose screw within
the machinery of my own body, I had been malfunctioning
without knowing it. How could a man live without feeling
his bones? I had missed everything.

Teste returned, we paid and, in the taxi taking us to the
airport where our plane for California waited, I leaned my
tense head on Teste's bony shoulder and watched the neon
of New York light up. It was going to be an idyll between
us, yes, sir. No one and nobody would come between us.

"How long are you going to stay, mon Teste?" I said.

Wordlessly, he pointed to the meter of the taxi which
was just then hovering between twenty-nine and thirty,
miles or dollars I don't know, and when thirty finally
became firm, he lowered his index finger. Ah, thirty . . .
But thirty what? Thirty days? Thirty weeks? Thirty years?
Thirty minutes?

"Thirty what?" I said. "Thirty days, thirty weeks, thirty
years, thirty minutes?"

"Thirty times," he said.

"Oh?!"

"I will stay until you have insulted me thirty times. Then
I will leave."

"I will never insult you, Monsieur Teste," I cried out.

"One," he said.

*

ON THE PLANE I kept silent, calculating feverishly the many

ways in which I would keep myself from insulting Teste. I would never refer to him without the polite Monsieur before his name. I would never talk politics. I would ignore the strangeness of his body. I would this and I would that. I had twenty-nine times left and I planned to use insults sparingly. I wanted Teste with me as long as possible. And if, I thought with cynical smugness, I got tired of him I can always insult him really fast twenty-nine times in a row and hasten his departure tremendously. But then I felt so guilty for allowing this thought to cross my sorry mind that I grimly clenched my smugness and pulled out a lock of my hair in self-retaliation. Teste was silent also. It was hard for me to tell whether he enjoyed the quiet night flight or whether he was listening to some internal rumbling. Before I could decide, the stewardess approached inside a teased platinum blond cloud and handed us glasses full of Coca Cola like red rain out of the fullness of her heart. I could have kissed and embraced her for her gesture but I refrained when I saw Monsieur purse his lips, close one eye, put the straw behind his ear and spill the Coke. If I hadn't seen the deliberateness of it I might have thought the incident accidental. But I was sure he had done it on purpose. Why? To make me insult him? Absurd! Presently, the platinum blond cloud folded in neat halves and two white branches shot out of her plumpness and began groping blindly at my feet with a yellow paper towel, the end of which looked like a sail and, suddenly, I understood! Monsieur had created the incident in order to make me see that other things beside platinum clouds filled with red raindrops existed. There were, in this marvelous world, also platinum blond clouds filled with red rain navigating at our feet with yellow sails. Oh, Teste!

Not much else happened on the plane and soon we saw the blue lights of San Francisco carpeting the earth like a cemetery of fresh ghosts signalling to the stars which were, you've guessed it, us.

Ah, what times awaited us! What mounds of blueberries! What terrors of filament! What corrections! What complete misuse! What tremendous erections! What filmy collaterals! What love! What caprice! What torrents! What torrential injections! What adjectives! What perceptions! Raining upward, the lights of San Francisco filled me with the elan of a god whose immortality rests in insults! A human whose love depends on a shut mouth! A monster whose ears must stay open all the time! A Lilliputian tied to the head sperm in the spermpack of a giant about to shoot his load in the belly of time! What felicity!

*

THE COFFEE was cozily percolating, the sunlight lanced the dust motes in the air. We were sitting on the rug, in my pleasant little San Francisco apartment (I keep one in the city), Teste and I, exchanging significant glances though their significance was vastly increased, no doubt, by my interpretations of them. I read a thousand meanings in his slightest movement and each one of these meanings enriched my life enormously, inexplicably. When, finally, we decided to talk it was at a level decidedly lower than the one I had just experienced.

"What's your watch worth?" I said, noticing an expensive gold watch on his wrist.

"It is the most expensive watch in the world," he said. "It is my one and only admission that the world exists. An expensive admission. One must never admit anything, but if one has no choice, as in the case of time, one must not admit cheaply."

"An admission is an admission," I said. "What does it matter if the signature under a man's confession is set with diamonds or not? He has confessed, that's all."

"You are wrong, *mon chou*. If a man could sign his confession in diamonds he would lend magnificence to his admission. He should, at least, sign with great care and a feeling of the absolute."

"Value," he continued, "is a defense of the unattainable. All things must be expensive. Things are an admission of man's impotence. They must not come cheap."

"The people are poor," I said.

"The people are bored," replied Monsieur.

"At least they aren't private," I countered.

He thought about this for a moment then reminded me of a fact I had forgotten:

"I am minding my own business."

With great pleasure I proceeded to describe to him how minding one's own business was not possible in America and how this wasn't really a bad thing because while it was true that others delved into one's business it was also possible for one to delve into others' business and *that*, you will grant, is the supreme pleasure of a democracy.

"What about music?" he cried. "And dance?"

"That is true," I readily agreed. "In America all art forms are in the service of literature. Their job is to fatten up the words."

I showed him gorgeously illustrated art and music magazines in which the language, obviously inspired by the fact that no one had been there before, took off in fat and happy ways, exploding here and there around a comma only to redress itself and masturbate endlessly. I showed him dancers kneeling before reviews of their own work as if seeing themselves in a mirror for the first time. There was no endeavor, creative or crafty, that did not aim its crippled heart at the dartboard of print.

Monsieur Teste showed no sign that he saw what I was showing him. He said, "These people speak in complete sentences!"

There was so much contempt in his voice. I did not understand.

"The infinite," he said, "is a great influence on unfinished sentences."

That is true. I had been blind. Infinity was demanding my apologies. I turned toward the coffee maker which sat on the window sill and, looking vaguely at the gorgeous clouds, I murmured my excuses.

*

April 16, 1974

I MASTURBATED as I got up. Monsieur Teste said:

"You are getting old. Instead of strangers, you fantasize about great lays of yesteryear."

"I beg your pardon," I said. "There was, in all those lays, a stranger I hadn't noticed at the time."

At breakfast, Monsieur Teste had a raw egg and a carrot. I asked him why.

"Entrusting your discoveries to language is like giving information to the wrong spy."

"But how else could you answer my question?"

Swiftly, he half-rose from his chair and plopped the yet uneaten raw egg into my face while, with his other hand, he thrust the carrot in my mouth which had fallen open from shock and surprise.

I told him, as I wiped off the goo, that it's possible to fool the language without resorting to action. He looked at me contemptously and got himself another egg from the refrigerator which he left open to stare into for the rest of his breakfast.

During the afternoon, I was so exhilarated to have him unveil the simple secrets of America for me, that I told him, "This will be a fruitful time for me. Thank you."

"In the first place," he said, "don't ever thank me. The Japanese have seven ways of saying 'thank you' and each one implies a certain degree of resentment. In the second place," he continued, "I like the word 'fruitful.'"

He proceeded to tell me the story of a conference he had once participated in. "After having said many things to each other during the conference, the gentlemen bowed their various heads and took off for parts unknown, some to bus stations and some to little restaurants in the neighborhood.

"It had not been a lost day. It had been fruitful and each and everyone carried the fruit of it in his heart. Some carried pears, others carried figs, others draped limp bananas over their biceps while yet others could be seen with mangoes. 'Seen,' that is, through the look in their eyes. But the hearts these gentlemen carried inside were all identical. Each heart carried four chambers and each chamber was loaded with fruit.

"When the gentlemen played Russian roulette, later that afternoon, they aimed their hearts at their heads before squeezing the trigger. Death, for the winners, consisted in fruit taking root in the brain. 'Life is a fruit in the heart of a targeted brain' was the motto of this session. Death, therefore, is a last minute rush for vitamins.

"Every time a fruitful conference takes place the gentlemen age a little and this conference was no exception. It seemed that other gentlemen's emanations made the gentlemen older. If the gentlemen could be left alone from birth to death, aging would not occur. But nobody grants the gentlemen solitude, least of all the gentlemen themselves. So the gentlemen want to be wolves. Can you blame them?"

"My God," I said, "it occurs to me that information works for death."

"A hired hand, cher."

"But what was the subject of this conference?"

Monsieur Teste lit a cigarette, looked at me with undisguised pity and said, "Anyone found frowning on the new god Chemistry will not be pulled out of the crucible in time for the party." Then slowly, he added, "Two."

✳

April 17
I HAD a horrendous dream last night. I dreamt that Mon-

sieur Teste wasn't real. I was terrified. But then the following solution offered itself to me: *Unreal people never ex-
cercise benevolence. They exist in the interim.*

There was a poem in the newspaper today. Monsieur and
I read it together:

> *It's tough to be doing what you don't*
> *find easy*
> *it's easy it's really easy*
> *to do what you want*
> *the body takes the lead*
> *over the head*
> *the heart swings the whip*
> *the body is hip*
> *the head is dead*

   I expected Teste to fly out in a rage. "Teste" means *head*
(in my opinion) and I thought the poem insulted this part
of the body. Instead, Teste was rather pleased. He said
that Teste does not mean *head* and it never meant *testes*
but it will always mean *taste*.

I thought I noticed a spark of eroticism in Teste. But I was
mistaken. He was merely sticking his tongue in and out of
his mouth to see how far it would go.

Last night, as we lay on our bunks, Monsieur Teste told
me his opinion of truth. He told me of the high regard he
had for the truth. It is precisely because of this regard that
he lied all the time. But, in his own words:
   "I lie in order to hide the truth from morons. It's the
morons I have to keep in the dark. Did you ever notice that
when a moron steps into the light from a, let's say, dark
room the light doesn't seem to matter any more. The
moron brings the darkness with him. All morons carry
dark rooms. Why did the moron tiptoe past the medicine

cabinet? There are people who claim that enlightening the morons is the greatest thing anyone can do. These people are morons themselves. Crypto-morons. And it's because there are crypto-morons around that one has to hide the truth at all cost. The crypto-morons love to get to the truth in order to pass it on to the obvious morons who then proceed to draw conclusions. This is how you can tell a moron from a non-moron. The morons always draw conclusions. Whenever there are more than three humans in a room the moron among them will reveal himself by drawing conclusions. This is all detailed in my pamphlet: *How to Catch a Moron.* Some morons are so eager to draw conclusions that they don't even wait for something to draw conclusions from. They pull them out of thin air. These particular morons are not dangerous. They draw their conclusions and, if left alone, they will not bother anybody. But if they have even a single fan, watch out! It's the morons who work over a bit of material, however, that are to be most feared. Scientists are the foremost example of this type of moron. . . ."

*

April 18
I MUST ADMIT, after he'd gone to sleep, I became worried about Monsieur Teste. He might not survive his sojourn in America. He'd barely been here five days and he had already begun to abandon large portions of the language. I could not for example, induce Teste to say "Pepsi." That he hadn't yet abandoned the entire American language was due, no doubt, only to the resiliency of a few abstract words for sentiment which weren't much in vogue and on the backs of which Teste hoped to slide unobserved by the everawake collectivism of the language.

"Don't worry," Teste said when I dropped my angst on him next day. "My real ally is the resiliency of subjunctives. I am not, properly speaking, abandoning the language, I am merely watching the language abandon itself after it passes through the torture chamber in my lower belly."

Good for the subjunctives! They had a lot of nerve. I would hate to lose Teste at this critical stage in our relationship.

He didn't say a word all afternoon. We took a walk and, thinking to please him, I pointed out several objects and repeated their names like a child: "Trolley car. Salami. Chevrolet."

I knew what he was thinking. He thought that I was deliberately setting out to destroy the uniqueness of objects by naming them.

When we got home he gave me a demonstration of how to deal with names. He pointed to the coffee maker and said "floor," to the fruit-bowl and said "foot." Then he looked smug and satisfied. Since there were no morons around I felt insulted. I'm not a moron. I know a fruit bowl from a foot. The strangeness of our state hit me. Here I was, stepping lightly through polysyllables in order not to insult him and with every insult he dealt me I felt myself to be more and more successful. The more he insulted *me* the less capable I was of insulting *him*. He was denying the laws of communication.

In the evening we had visitors. The swinger couple Johnson. The two of them are the embodied American principle: Both Sides Of The Question. This principle, taken from television, took in the Johnsons the appalling form of a tremendously fast rush to make decisions followed immediately by counter-decisions. An evening with the Johnsons amounted to nothing in the end because as soon as the Johnsons did something they analyzed it instantly. They were swingers who swung away from each other. As soon as the male Johnson took off his clothes, the female Johnson put on her coat, and, as neither Teste nor I did anything, he hastily put his clothes back on as the female Johnson walked out of hers. As soon as she took her clothes off I took off mine and looked as she put hers back on only to be followed by the male Johnson dutifully taking his off at which point I put mine back on and watched as the process swung inevitably toward futility, all this time keeping an eye on Teste who opened the refrigerator door and began what now amounted to an addiction with him: staring into the depths of it.

It was, I thought, a delightful way to spend an evening but Monsieur thought differently:

"You've been doing the wrong thing," he said to me. "You've been trying to be human. It is better to be a root or a stalk. The point is that you can't trust the world with your understanding of it."

"But how then," I said in utter astonishment, "can you entrust the world to your understanding?"

"You can't," he said and laughed — the first time I have ever seen him laughing because, if you remember, he never laughed with Valéry.

In the middle of the night I got up, careful not to wake Monsieur, and I began to write in my journal. But he woke up and spoiled my pleasure.

"Aha!" he said. "You don't believe that the world exists!"

"What do you mean?" I feigned, knowing only too well what he meant.

"Writing stands squarely in opposition to the world; it is an addition to perception, an ordering process, a way of forcing unnatural connections, it is an inaccurate description for the sake of sanity . . . You're afraid of going mad . . . You think that you're allowing visions to surface while in reality you are putting a verbal lid on your unconscious . . . You are perpetuating a system on which the mind bases its arrogance against nature. . . ."

He was absolutely right. I burnt my notebook.

*

April 19

AMERICAN POETRY came to lunch today. Many poets were missing but I made do with the ones who were there. The poets there were mostly from the New York School, a school which I attended in the hope of finding out the simple secrets the ignorance of which so handicaps a foreigner in America. These poets knew a great number of simple secrets which they spread around generously, unlike the rest of the schools which bored me to death with their European pretentions. I had learned, among others, such notions as "Clear the range!" (Ted Berrigan), "If it fits in your mouth, it's natural!" (Ted Berrigan), "Take it easy!" (Anne Waldman), "What's up, Doc?" (Tom Veitch), "Why not Egypt?" (Dick Gallup).

For lunch I cooked a whole favorite menu of mine composed of fifteen dishes:

ENTREE
New poetry movements. (I am an expert in these because I made up most of them. Aktup, Metabolism, the Bowel Movement and Syllogism. All have me as one of the founders. I have also furthered Actualism, Essentialism and Infantilism. American poets, with their pragmatic sense of craft and their ferocious drive toward respectability, are afraid of labels. This is because labels, traditionally, have been put on them by critics. So, at some point in American poetry, there began a race to elude critics. The widest range of cultural eclecticism was brought into play in every poem in order that the poet place him or herself beyond criticism. The exceptions to this are the conceptually inclined, who paste on their own labels and elaborate their philosophy at leisure. See Isidore Isou's Lettrisme through to Aram Saroyan's Minimalism.)

SOUP
Pure meaninglessness does not exist, only misdirected in-

tentions. Nobody has yet written a perfectly obscure poem.
Sit down, Clark Coolidge. Is it because nobody has yet committed a perfectly arbitrary act? I would think that a complete
student of the abstract does not exist either, because he or she
would have a body, hence a cliche. In the form of a body
everybody inhabits a cliche. The question, naturally, is: Is the
Universe arbitrary? And the answer, depending on your prej-
dices, commits you to a cliche. But nothing, *nothing* can stop
you from reshuffling it, regardless of point of view.

PÂTÉ DE FOIE GRAS
Ted Berrigan and Tom Veitch.

Ted Berrigan (who has Dada and is basically innocent)
reshuffles the language we speak every day in order to present
himself to us disguised as us, but from an unexpected angle,
that of hearing our own words in his mouth on a page cut in
talk patterns. Tom Veitch (who has God and is essentially
anxious) reshuffles concepts like death, love and sex in order
that they leave their conceptual skins to throw us into fits of
self-examination. Tom uses a lofty and aristocratic place from
which things are small enough to be manipulated but big
enough to scare the wits out of us. Ted, on the contrary, is
possessed by one instrument, his voice. Ted is a purer writer
than Tom because the philosophy of a situation only interests
him if it is incomplete, i.e., human. Tom reaches for harmony
with higher forces and is, in this sense, a magician. Purity, one
sees, is really the degree of dedication to one's obsession. Ted
is obsessed with voice, Tom with God, and each of them does
it by shifting things out of their conventional places.

GRAVY
I see reality through a grid.
Each little square in the grid is an action
preceded by DON'T.
Outside the grid is the world of DO
so if I were looking in from the outside
I would be so busy I wouldn't even
perceive the grid
hence no poems.

A MEDIUM-SIZED SUCKLING PIG WITH AN APPLE IN HIS MOUTH
There are poets with a distaste for reality.

These poets are insane, meaning that they have no defined
territory toward which to reshuffle their world, so they
wander through their imaginations and bring out things that,
on first sight, nobody has ever seen. These poets have to be
intelligent, however, and if they are, they usually notice that
what they brought back resembles some quite common thing
that everybody sees every day. At this point, they form a
method by bringing intelligence to bear on romanticism.
These poets have no style. They are mechanics of celestial
pornography. Michael Brownstein is one of these. I have
never seen anything of his in which a subtle apology isn't
made to some secret search. All his works say: *Look, I am
sorry, dear God, but as I was coming through the stratosphere
half of you burned up so I put a shoe in the missing place.*
John Ashbery does the same thing but he keeps his terms
abstract. This is a terrible disadvantage because abstracts tend
to make one re-examine one's shakiest assumptions and, if
this were done, it would take twelve years to correctly read
a John Ashbery poem.

STEAMING SPUDS
The search for meaning is an instinct, especially if the poem
suggests that meaning should occur. But no poem, as said
before, can help *but* suggest it, because language is a machine
of control. The language of poets like Brownstein and
Ashbery is, usually, international. The Surrealists were of the
same mind and ended up creating the first international poetry
idiom.

FRUIT: PEACHES, MELONS AND BLACKBERRIES
It is a monument to the stupidity of American criticism that
all references to the New York School have, so far, spoken of
a collective voice when, in truth, it is precisely the New York
School that has brought the largest number of methods, attitudes and trends into a scene dominated by uniformity and
boredom. There are at least fifteen poets in this set who em-
body essentially fifteen major philosophies.

DRUGS: COCAINE, YOGA AND POT
The politico-literal-sexual waterfall of Anne Waldman, John
Giorno, Tom Clark and Lewis MacAdams. In this case, the
personalities of the poets are in constant demand and the

steady intensity becomes a special therapy, models of which could be made and sold at political conventions.

NAPOLEONS, RHUM BABAS, ECLAIRS AND BAKLAVA
Informational accumulation in view of a massive collapse of the senses; Peter Schjeldahl's monomaniacal recording of dreams, Scott Cohen's fascination with large statistics, Alice Notley's collection of bizarre colors and rare flowers, Kenneth Koch's lyrical efforts to eat the vocabulary, etc.

CIGARS
Aram Saroyan and Joyce Holland. Minimalism and Essentialism.

COFFEE
The wonder world of Joe Brainard. This is the LOOK WHAT I FOUND! school and is, uniquely, American.

HONEY
A school of cultural refinement organized around obscure but exciting quarrels with all kinds of Alexandrian poses, eclectic decadence and transcendental irony. (Transcendental irony is, naturally, the opposite of bourgeois or proletarian irony. It is irony with the superior term in another world.) Tony Towle, Carter Ratcliff, Ron Padgett (sometimes), Kenward Elmslie, Bill Berkson.

A FINAL JOINT
None of these exist in a pure state. See Dick Gallup.

WHIPPED CREAM
There is a lot more. Some resident critics would now be in order. Poets, as a rule, see themselves as defined by their works and the critical intelligence brought to bear on their contemporaries is almost always oral. America is, however, in great need of some new directions and a translation of these poetries into easy-to-follow computer programs could, conceivably, save the world a hundred years of sterility.

Everybody relished the food immensely and when we were all full, we began to sing songs made on the spur of the moment and write collaborations.

Later, Teste and I washed the enormous pile of dishes

in silence. Throughout the evening, Teste had been terribly quiet, unimpressed with all the gaiety around him. I did not want to press him for an opinion of the evening but, shortly after, he said, "I find collaboration like youth: chatty and arrogant."

Pressed for clarification, Monsieur said the following (which I am going to use as an introduction to the collaborations of the previous evening): "As the Nazis knew, collaboration helps the Empire. It is a sad reflection on our times that instead of fucking, people collaborate. Do you know how many drugs you consumed last night?"

"No," I said, "I don't remember."

"The hipper among your readers . . ."

"The *hipper*?!"

"The heap there, of readers, will, no doubt, be able to identify what drugs went into each one of these sad works and, god knows, there was hashish, speed, coke, opium in alcohol, alcohol in glasses, etc., going in at the rate of two grams per poem."

"The Surrealists," I said, "like the late New York School . . ."

"Ended up dead and in books."

"Collaboration was quite the rage in Alexandria too in the sixth century . . . Alexandrine verse originated in two heads . . ."

"Which goes to prove that, being homosexual, the great Alexandrine writers convinced the better-looking boys to pick up the warm pen and finish their thoughts . . ."

Teste smirked and, without apparent connection, added savagely, "I am *not* from Rumania."

"Each one's Teste is from wherever each one is," I said, but he didn't laugh.

"I am an embodiment of the third person," he said.

"The hell you are," I countered. "You're the second or nothing."

We had our first quarrel.

"Big words are the mark of small minds," he said.

"Up your ass."

Tonight we made up. We looked at the immense sky filled with stars and felt at peace with each other. Teste did not need any prompting to feel at peace but I had to repeat to myself William Carlos Williams' famous lines:

I have discovered that most of
the beauties of travel are due to
the strange hours we keep to see them

before I too felt a cosmic grace and boundless happiness. My heart, at 3 A.M. was full and in harmony.

*

April 20
THIS MORNING I realized the difference between me and Teste. He is at least twenty years older than I am because he is French. I overheard him murmuring, as he was shaving: "Understanding is for old folks. Young ones should fight."
I can't say I disagree. But can you trust the old fogies?

"Being as full of ideas as you are," said Monsieur, disdainfully, "you will not have failed to notice that I never think about sex."
"I have noticed," I answered curtly. "At your age . . . I understand . . ."
"You understand nothing. I am the opposite of sex."

We went to the ocean.
"Isn't it beautiful?" I said.
"No," growled Teste. "It's obvious. I like my beauty elusive, a little perverse if you please . . ."

I was beginning to wish Teste would leave. Slowly, a hooded executioner rose from my archetypal pool bearing the shiny tools of his trade: insults, conspiracies and anxiety. I knew, however, that I could not, at this time, execute

Teste without eliminating myself in the bargain. I pro-
posed a vacation instead.

To my surprise, Monsieur agreed. He was already taking
walks by himself, he would simply prolong one of these and
walk for a whole day and night. He packed up very
carefully the three items he carried and left without words.

*

April 21

A BLISSFUL DAY. Not a thought. I had steak and eggs for
breakfast.

*

April 22

"MONEY," I SAID. "Money, Teste." He didn't understand. "I
can't afford to keep you any longer. I ran out of money."

Teste regarded me, squinting: "What you mean to say
is, you are afraid of what I *think* about money?"

"I know you *don't* think about money. You merely understand its principles. You know, for example, how it oper-
ates, what it's used for and how it can be transfered from
one pile onto another. You are a brilliant economist, Teste,
but what I'm saying is: I don't have a penny. We need cash."

"OK," said Teste. "Here is what you do. You go into a
big department store and buy a steam iron or a power
drill. You pay for these, go to your car, put the drill or the
iron on the front seat and then return to the store with
your bag and receipt. In there you get another steam iron
power drill, walk up to the cashier and say, 'I'm sorry. I
just remembered that I already have one. I would like my
money back. Unfortunately, I don't seem able to find the
receipt. But you remember me, I was here a moment ago.'
She'll give you money; you go back to your car and drive
your iron or drill to a similar department store where,
since you have the receipt, you can get more money."

I was astonished. Monsieur Teste, Monsieur Teste, where did you pick up that kind of detail? That is utterly unlike you. "I picked that up," said Teste in answer to my thoughts, "in Monterey. I like scams. Scams are forms of relaxation."

And think of it, only yesterday I had been tired of him. And today, today, he started talking native. Simple secrets, "scams" he calls them. Our relationship was squarely back to its original purpose: accelerating my enjoyment of simple secrets. Which is not to say that Monsieur Teste is practical. He is not. He is an aristocrat. I must describe his face in case you missed him: like a doll torn up by traffic, his face bears the scars of a thousand typewriters. But over it, a sort of plastic mold has settled, fixing his features in place, a mask of serenity. An aristocrat does not move without reason. I need Teste. He is the logic of my childhood. I must defend my life from prose.

"Which direction should we go?" I asked him in the morning as we were about to take a rare common walk.

A cement mixer, across the street, began its infernal whirring. Monsieur listened intently.

"It sounds like it wants to hurl us north."

Monsieur liked to leave the impression that his decisions were dictated by the advice of inanimate objects in his surroundings. Perhaps they were. After all, he had *really* listened to that cement mixer.

Teste has a vast understanding of literature. Like a cement mixer his mind can hurl together disparate fragments of various books to create the continuous paste of interest on which his presence is founded. People always ask him, he told me, how is it that he loves writers that he, only a week before, castigated for cheapness and stupidity. That is, Monsieur Teste replies, because a week ago he hadn't read them. "I was castigating them for not coming to my attention. There is no reason in the world why I should love somebody I never read!"

He generally manages to give a psychological slant to his knowledge, which is a pity, really, considering that what makes reading great is lack of editorial attitudes. We quarrelled over fiction. Fiction, in my opinion, should divest itself of psychology. Description is really psychology so, please, no description. Dialogue is generally nonsense so, please, don't say anything.

What remains then? Why, the subjunctives, of course.

Teste heartily agreed but said this: "Do you like people or not?"

"Well, I do, sort of . . . of course . . ."

"There you are," he said. "You need psychology to eliminate the threat to your reputation."

I really don't know what to make of Teste. On one hand he says that it is better to be a root or a stalk. On the other he recognizes the human dimension. Then I remembered what he thinks of writing, in general, and I realized: my God, he is tremendously real, he is over-real, he is here and oh, perhaps he has no plan, after all.

I was mad. But Teste had already curled up in a chair, with the refrigerator door open, staring into what to him must have amounted to the heart of Universe.

*

April 23

I WOKE in panic. I thought, for a moment, that Teste had packed his swift bag and left in the middle of the night. I was happy to hear him say, "Your genes are like the layers of an onion. None of your ancestors had enough imagination to make himself God."

"Actually," I began tentatively, "my grandmother . . ."

"Cut the crap," he said. "There is no purposefulness in you."

"You mean purpose?"

"No. I mean 'purposefulness' like stature. I have watched you get up in the morning. Every morning is different. Sometimes you wake up feet first, sometimes you lift your head up and, at times, you feel the air with your hand like a cheap viola in search of a Nazi."

"You mean — no consistency?"

"I mean well," he said.

"And yet," I replied, pointing to the piles of manuscripts lining the tops of our heads on shelves set high enough so the cat wouldn't piss on them, "there is consistency in those. I want to tell the world about the prejudices of my time and how my personality reacted to them."

"Ha ha ha," said Teste, "you don't even claim resistance. Or distance. You are a lost soul."

Looking like a bishop, Monsieur joined his hands and put the mitre of his tangled fingers in my face. They smelt, slightly, of garlic and asparagus.

In order to prove my humanity, consistency and reality I worked all afternoon on a *Dictionary of Received Ideas* to spring on Teste when he returned from the walk he had now gotten into the consistent habit of taking by himself.

I quote from the rather lengthy work:

If you look at fire long you'll pee in bed.
The underground's been forced there by mean weights.
The excess of reason makes monsters of boredom.
White flowers are funereal.
Black flowers are erotic.
The academia is taxation without imagination.
Carfax Anthrax.
God is partial to ferociousness.
Birds filled wtih lead.
A sense of humor is a sense of authority.
Closeups don't have any sense of humor.
Truth sits in an autobiography like a bird dog in an
underground hospital.
The Exterminator is after the facts.

A man's name is his cage.
A miracle is the shortest explanation.
Intuition is the daughter of miracles.
Baby irony is transcendental.
Geriatric irony is worldly.
Worlds meet at ironic junctions: the resulting clash is a
miracle.
Mommy means I want, Money means I don't need her.
Heraldry is structural horniness.
The penis is a barricade.
Poetry is mistranslation.
A discovery is followed by silence not applause.

I wrote hundreds of these but when Teste came home I didn't dare show them to him for fear he would open the refrigerator door and say nothing. Teste is not rude, he is just superior. Without him, I wouldn't even know there are better things in this world.

Teste is a gourmet. I won't mention all the things he brings home from his walks: fragments of old fire escapes, snails without shells (slugs), dirty socks, meteors.

*

April 24
TODAY, AS TESTE lay silently on his bunk looking at an incipient spiderweb, I planted myself by the door and broached the subject of insults. Every day since he had arrived, I had become more and more insulting, yet he did not seem to notice. I had broken my own rules a hundred times. I had done him endless little bad turns. I had made him gulp America while I held his jaws open. I had been a miserable tormentor to this man whose sublime dislike of history made him a saint. I had been horrible and yet, like a flower enjoying the crassness of a florist, he had withstood my grossness with a lighter and lighter heart. He must like it here, I thought. And if he does it will be *I* who must move

out . . . I am the one carrying dissatisfaction. Teste is spotless. He has grown more real while I have grown more insecure.

I blurted, "Teste, mon cher, I think it is impossible for me to insult you."

"You will find a way," he said.

"I'm stuffed up with thoughts like a swan with pomegranates," I confessed.

Feigning innocence, which he despised, he said: "You sure know your Latin!"

The funniest thing happened. Teste was coming home when, suddenly, two burly men grabbed his thin arms, pushed him into a doorway and emptied his pockets. He had nothing on him except the mathematical instrument at the bottom of the little velvet case in his vest pocket.

"What's this?" one of the men said, holding the tiny tentacles of solid brass to the street light.

"Allow me," said Teste. He took the instrument from the man's hand and began turning the black tentacles.

"Hey," said the other man, "I hope that thing ain't . . ."

He finished with a howl of pain. His companion began to also howl and as they howled Teste stepped neatly through the thin part in the middle of their pain loop and exited into the sunlight where a wino greeted him.

"How did you do it?" I asked.

"Simple," said Teste. "They were looking into my eyes."

"And?"

"They understood."

*

April 25

I HAVE CHANCED upon the ultimate insult. I will put Monsieur Teste in a novel. It had been Paul Valéry's way of subduing his Teste and I have no proof that it won't work.

I mapped my attack or "my novel." My novel would

have no relationships. This is difficult since not only characters but also words stand in certain relationships to each other. It is in the nature of relationships to delegate ownership to the wrong party. Of course, only *natural* relationships are at ease with their possessions. *Unnatural* relationships are insecure and therefore amenable to my eventual dismantling of their territories. Could there possibly be unnatural relationships between characters that know each other? No. Their acquaintance legitimizes their relationship. The first rule of my novel would be then: the characters must not know each other. The way to do this is to hide them from each other in ways too ingenious for them to discover. What is the most ingenious thing on earth? Ah, the Cathedrals, of course. They are unsurpassed in ingenuity. I will build my novel like a cathedral and I will place my characters at the intersection points of the naves on elliptical orbits so that no matter how hard they try they cannot intersect. I will then place Monsieur Teste at a corner of a north inner square so that he can look up and see the whole circle of characters above but will not be able to reach them until the circle is squared. And that, I knew, would take a while.

What an insult!

*

April 26

THE STRUCTURAL DESIGN I was looking for was printed in an old *National Geographic*. I was studying it at breakfast this morning when Teste, with uncharacteristic curiosity, peered at it.

"Ha ha ha," he laughed, "I see that you've reached Point Terminus."

I said nothing.

"I will tell you a parable. A rich man had a servant who annoyed him. The rich man could not very well kill his servant because he was a civilized rich man and he abhorred strong-arm methods."

"Hmmm."

"So he decided to take his servant with him for a visit to the Labyrinth in Crete where the minotaur was imprisoned. He planned to lose his servant in the labyrinth. If the man could not find the exit he would blame his own stupidity."

"Right," I said, guessing the end. "The servant got out, but the rich man was lost."

"Wrong," said Teste. "They were lost together and had to keep each other company until they died."

Ugh! I at once scrapped the idea of losing Monsieur in a novel. I recognized the parable.

THE BIG CHANGE

AT THIS POINT I will dispense with dates because the subsequent events did not belong to time, *do* not belong to time. Roughly, The Big Change would, if the chroniclers insist, last between April 27 and March 6, making Monsieur Teste's American sojourn exactly twenty-one days long, but I must say to the chroniclers' eternal confusion that not only does time have nothing to do with it but neither do I or Teste for that matter.

I prepared The Big Change with the thoroughness of a fat student preparing for a diet exam. For weeks, just under the skin of my consciousness, my chemistry prepared to flood the outline of the world with a dazzling substance. On April 28, the outline was filled, time evacuated the chamber like hydrogen escaping the balloon and The Big Change reared nervously in readiness.

Since my identification papers were in the disorder proper to a shadowy alien I borrowed a friend's ID and credit card. Under his name I rented a car which I didn't know how to drive. I got behind the wheel and ignoring my ignorance I drove to the house, I packed Monsieur's bag (he was out walking) and I settled to wait for him as an invisible crayon drew black circles under my eyes. He returned at 6:15, stepping, as it were, straight out of a splendid San Francisco sunset painted by Alice C., circa 1970. "Entrez," I said, sliding the car door open like an involuntary wing. He entered and we were on our way. I turned on the car radio and this song escaped the FM band to complement the sunset, amplify my triumph and underscore Teste's feigned bewilderment:

> We're on our way
> Where to I couldn't say

We were going, I shouted to Monsieur, to the source of all my problems, to the place where boredom had nearly killed me, we were going to Heaven or, if you prefer, we were returning to the country in the wild depths of which my tree house stood with the lingering shape of the postmistress still darkening the window. We were going to the place where my cry for help had formed the telegram by means of which humans always telegraph their gods that they are in trouble.

I was taking Monsieur Teste to a place unlike any other: the countryside of northern California, that gothic slumber of prehistoric ferns slowly shaking their scales upward toward trees so tall the clouds had to tear their bellies going over, that place of mysterious murders, bodies floating down the swollen river, sudden red moons, hysterical and ancient inhabitants exchanging gasoline bombs with new but brutal settlers. We were going to the Wild Wild West, A.D. 1974, ad infinitum, ad nauseam, ad lib.

Up to this point, which was so small no light went through it, I had matched Teste's knowledge of the world bead by bead. I had been born in a city; Teste had, too. I had devised the coarse grains of my wit in coffee houses where Teste had his made into coffee, I had known sex in the shadow of libraries whose shadow Teste was, I had walked to the store at 4:00 A.M. for cigarettes as Teste had in the hope of being the first one to spot 5:00 A.M. as it dawned on the clock. Our experience, different as it may have been, had, until this point, sprung from a common landscape like a lion and a man from a formica sphinx. But now I was about to take Monsieur to the place where the crack first appeared on my soul map.

As the first signs of the country began to appear as ruined barns, stray dirigibles, hitchhikers, cows and enormous gold onions, I accelerated and at the speed of 150 miles per hour we effectuated our entry into this world.

A screech of brakes warned me that I had stopped for a hitchhiker.

She threw her gear in and swiftly followed suit.

"Where to?" I said.

"I don't care," said she, "as long as it's out of Sonoma County."

That, it was.

"American geography is bizarre," said Teste. "How can anyone go to a place the roads don't go to?"

"One can't," said I.

"You two," said the hitchhiker, "sound like grapes." I saw no connection but Monsieur did.

"We are grapes," said he.

"Don't get squashed," she said.

"We will," said Teste.

"I wish I was in love," said the hitchhiker. "I want to have a baby."

I care for love. I think that at the core of the universe a glowing lump of love sends its radiance through tremendous obstacles into our hearts.

"Do you have a baby?" Teste asked me, knowing only too well that I had no such thing.

"No."

I didn't have a baby. He didn't have a baby, of course.

"Will you have my baby?" I said to the hitchhiker.

"That depends."

"On whom?"

"On your stock," she said. "I will have nothing but the best stock."

"It's good stock," I said. "My ancestors were terribly particular about their stock, they even issued stock certificates on their continuing 99 per cent."

"What kind of stock?" she said.

"A rising stock."

"What's your stock?" she said to Monsieur who, throughout this exchange, had fallen asleep.

"I have no stock," replied Monsieur. "I come from nowhere. I'm a clear soup."

"Even clear soup is a stock," the perky vagabond said.

"What kind of stock," said Teste judiciously, "when it didn't even start with water but with ink?"

"Ink soup," she said, "Yeek."

"There you have it," I said, "I'm the sensible stock."

"OK," she said.

I was very happy. Now I would show Teste. I will have a baby in the totally baffling wilderness with an utter stranger. If he finds my reasons unimpeachable he will have to capitulate. And if he capitulates, I will stay in America, get my American citizenship and enlist in the army.

It was not to be.

We arrived, over tortuous roads, assiduous turns, pindrops, cliffhangers, curlicues, mud spirals, and twisted valley bottoms, to the little cabin which I had occupied until I had been seized by boredom. Faithfully, my dark cabin in the deep woods had kept itself for me wrapped for protection in vast networks of spider web. Everything was where it had been, ready to go to where it hadn't.

It hadn't, I am sure, been to the place where the three of us were soon to take it. It had never had more than one inhabitant and an occasional stranger. Its creaking floorboards had never supported the weight of three humans since the day it had been built. Its ceiling had never felt the warmth of three headtops, its walls had never been touched by six hands, its doorknobs had never been turned by thirty fingers, its one bed had never held three full heads of hair and its septic tank had never received an average of nineteen to twenty-seven bowel movements a week. But cabins, like question marks, have infinite patience. We felt at home. At least I did and Ellen, I am sure, did too. Teste had no home.

"Can imaginary characters have real babies?" a peasant once asked Voltaire.

"Of course," the great man said. "It's their way of facing reality."

*

First Night   (it is always night)
MONSIEUR TESTE makes a big fire in the woodstove, sits on the floor in front of it, folds in two and goes to sleep.

Ellen takes off her clothes. Her shadow is on the wall.

Her shadow on the wall is pierced by the stars in the window. Her flesh on the bed is pierced by the branch from my body. Flowers fall off and some fruit too.

The fire dies out. We sleep. The wind howls.

*

Second Night   (it is always night)
TESTE POINTS to the viciously full Scorpionic moon filling our little cabin window to the maximum, and says:

"Reason is an institution of the city like garbage trucks."

"Everything here is done to the maximum, Monsieur."

"MAXIMUM," shouts Ellen.

"What?"

"That's the name of our baby!"

"No," I say, "definitely not. He will carry the impossible on his passport."

"First of all it's a 'she,' second it's *my* baby."

"My stock."

"No," says Teste, "it's my baby."

"Huh?" Both Ellen and I stare at him as the stars pour in and we circle Teste considering where to bite.

"Yes," says Monsieur, "one can only have what one understands."

"Are you implying," I say, filling with bloodlust while a savage rhythm emanates from Ellen like a frenzied shaman drum, "that we don't know what we are doing?"

"We are human," I whisper viciously.

"We know love!" Ellen and I hiss in unison as the moon, unable to control itself any longer, breaks the window and fills the room with the torn-up cosmic shroud, enveloping Teste in a cold light in the midst of which he stands like a lock of hair in a gold medallion.

*

Third Night

MAXIMUM WAS BORN. It was an easy birth. I attended Ellen with half-pronounced words, comforting sounds, hisses and animal will. Teste did nothing. He looked into the fire ignoring the extraordinary physical and magical storm that had broken in the cabin. Even the trees outside rustled with the awareness of extraordinary events. A sudden rain fell. Animals pressed their warm bodies against the door. Maximum appeared head first so it was a while before we could tell its sex. It was a boy but something indefinite suggested a girl. A violin, its beginning shrouded in mystery, passed its bow through the exact center of my heart. I held the wet child in the moonlight.

"We have created a perfect hermaphrodite," Teste said.

I did not, at first, believe him, but as the night deepened and the exhausted mother fell asleep with Maximum on her chest, it began to dawn on me that, after all, Teste might be right.

Maximum had been born with silky black hair on its head, two oval eyes surveying a tiny yet unmistakably feminine mouth and its tiny nipples suggested already the inevitable blossoming forth of a female's breasts. So strong was the impression that, at once, I was swept off my feet by religious fervor and I thanked the forest for helping us produce our equivalent, as it were, of a unicorn. I knew that it was the wish of forests, of, indeed, the whole world of nature, to bring from its depths constant reaffirmations of its basic unity. These reaffirmations were continually frustrated by the tendency of things to view the world in terms of their dominant characteristics. Thus the obviousness of dominant characteristics carried the ball most of the time and definite pronouns were born into the world. But when dominant characteristics had their will turned off by a deep understanding of nature, the perfect came forth: the unicorn, the hermaphrodite.

It was something worth feeling mystical about, but Monsieur thought that god was a waste of energy. "You get a feeling of gratitude and what do you do with it? You throw it to the winds. Instead, you could be using it to make love."

"To make love with you?"

"No, no . . . Not 'make love' like 'fucking' but make love like wine out of grapes. Gratitude is a kind of wine grape. You squash it into your heart instead of wasting it in prayer and, lo and behold, there are thirty gallons of love."

"What other kinds of grapes . . . er . . . wine . . . love are there?"

"There are infinite varieties of love grapes depending on your innocence. There is, par exemple," continued Monsieur, looking into the fire which was now burning out, "the love grape called 'compassion.' This is a hard grape to make love from. It's also a hard grape to come by. This grape is usually found in weak old people who don't have the energy any longer to squeeze it for wine. There are professional grape squeezers who, even though they can't make love themselves, can help you squeeze these grapes. Then there is a kind of love grape called 'The Wonderful' and this makes champagne. The Wonderful is easy to come by but it's hard to see it when you do. The problem is, see, that The Wonderful does not flower in an average mentality."

"This is wonderful, Monsieur Teste," I said.

"Now take that unfinished prayer," he said, "and turn it back into your grateful heart where you have just caught The Wonderful and squeeze!"

I did what he said. I squeezed the love grape The Wonderful with all the might of the not inconsiderable weight of a half unspoken prayer. I don't think the pressure was nearly enough because love grape The Wonderful kept its juices.

"Harder, young fellow, harder!" bellowed Teste.

I threw my weight at the heart of the halfprayer and sank into The Wonderful like an ice-breaker and this time, yes, such a miracle, this time, yes, this time around oh The Wonderful popped its multiskins and exploded in a symphony of juice, leaving the arteries burning. Filled to the inside of my palate and soles with travelling love grape juice I could hear my hemoglobin already beginning to ferment it.

"How long before it's wine?" I asked breathlessly.

"Anywhere from thirty minutes to thirty years."

I sat there drowning in The Wonderful, keeping vigil over an intensely satisfied and peacefully sleeping female and a marvelous hermaphrodite. I stood vigil all night and, in the morning, when the first rays of the sun touched the face of the mother awakening her, I felt the beginnings of wine or love, if you prefer, stirring in the millions of bottles in my body.

Maximum awoke and stared vaguely at it.

*

Fourth Night
WE FOUND a fifteen-year-old child in the woods. He wore
nothing but a loincloth and from his appearance it was evi-
dent that he had been raised by savage animals. The wild
child avoided us at first, following us from a safe distance,
but when Teste brought forth his box of graham crackers
the child leaped in front of him and pulled the box from
his hands. At the cabin we washed him and from behind
the grime a most beautiful face appeared. The wild child
had an oval face surmounted by two brilliant eyes selected
by Goya. His mouth had been picked by El Greco and his
arms and legs had been ripped from Pericles statues and
blended into the art deco flawlessness of a torso molded by
Beardsley. He was, in one word, perfect. He was so terribly sensual, the window molding began to melt and, at
his slightest gesture, the pots and the plates floated gently
from their shelves and landed at an angle on the softest
minutes of dust. He exuded harmony. His breasts com-
plemented his male organ with a subtle blending of tex-
tures. Merely by touching it I had an indescribable
orgasm. An angelic faintness overtook me.

Then the wild child spoke in accents which could have
been learned at the court of King Arthur, "My name is
Maximum [he pronounced this in Latin, accent on the second syllable]. My father is a shiny vegetable who attained,
at the moment of my conception, an unbreakable nature
and turned into a shiny mineral. My mother is a believer
in 'Ask and ye shall receive' and she has made the treachery
of the interested ? into the main factor of her life. My uncle
Oscar, on the other hand, gives me all the candy I want
and takes me up and down in ship cruises across
marvelous territories. He makes quite a bit of money in the
process because I am a prostitute-saint and in some ports

they have built effigies of me and people fight for the right
to touch my private parts."

Everything became clear to me now. Teste had taken my
child to foreign countries and had pimped him out. I was
furious. I turned at once to face Monsieur with a wrench
in my hand. He looked at me through half-open lids. He looked at
me abstractly, he looked at me quizzically. I put the
wrench down and took refuge in a mean thought. Teste is
not important any longer. What, with all the responsibility
I now have to raise my child and the financial considera-
tions issuing therefrom, I can't possibly have any further
use for Teste. He was revoked. An apple wormed through
and through. A name on an expired passport. A question
mark in a field of daisies. He never did any work! He was
a pimp!

It was very late at night. I slept huddled next to the wild
child we found in the woods and I had countless orgasms.

*

Fifth Night
THE NATIVES CAME. They came softly, almost invisible at
first. They surrounded the house quietly like guerrillas.
Then some of the more courageous ones came inside. They
were, in general, a highly inarticulate bunch with fear
written on their faces. They made one think of the
distorted mailing labels that come out of a fouled linotype.
Behind them, other natives, armed with pitchforks and
grins of such stupidity it was hard to believe one's eyes,
gushed forth amidst a geyser of proto-syllables.

They had come to see Maximum. I showed it to them
as it lay there sound asleep on the small bed. They didn't
see it.

"Is he shitting us?" said the fireman to Teste who was ignoring him.

"Isee eveh!" hissed the postmistress.

"Gentlemen," said Teste, "I think you must be warned that I deal roughly with impolite punks."

"He does," I hastened to affirm, "he really does."

"Yeah," said the fireman, clicking his spurs and disengaging the steel axe from his belt, "let's see, focker!" Teste extracted a glowing coal from the stove and threw it in the fireman's face who immediately began to roll on the floor, his eyes glowing, a three-alarm fire beginning in his body. Maximum awoke and, seeing what was happening, shouted, "UNCLE O!" jumping, at the same time, on the auto mechanic's back, pulling, with an expert gesture, a little lid. Gas gushed out of the man's body, felling him.

The rest of the natives suddenly raised their eyes upward and falling on their knees began a heart-rending *Te Deum*. They had seen Maximum.

"The lower organisms," said Teste "can see only if their sight is awaken by violence."

It was true, of course. Still, I prefer peace to pedagogy.

*

Sixth Night

ELLEN RETURNED. At midnight. The day after the birth of her child she had gone into space.

I told her how Teste had pimped out our child, how the natives had come, how I felt and what I wanted. I told her, in short, of history.

"No, no," she said, "it was I who, disguised as Uncle Oscar, sold our child for pennies in foreign ports."

"Impossible," I exclaimed, "it would be inconsistent with your character."

"Character, my ass. Men always think that women exist to listen to history. I despise history. I have inconsistencies. I am human."

"There are no inconsistencies," Teste butted in. "Inconsistencies are new characters."

"Which is what we need around here," said Ellen ominously. "Some new characters."

I could not stop what happened next. Ellen rose above Teste like a giant bird. Monsieur withstood the assault with aplomb by making himself entirely malleable like soft tar. Ellen began to mold him. She made crenellated punch craters in his chest, she twisted his nose so that the tip of it ended between his eyes, she put his ears on his nipples, she emptied his eye sockets and put the eyeballs in his scrotum, she split his penis in two and put each portion in one of the eye sockets, she wove his legs and arms in an Inca blanket of vast dimensions, she shuffled his hips and in each of his bones she planted a different flower, she did other minor and major adjustments until the proud figure of the sad European aristocrat looked exactly like the potbellied stove in which the faint fire stirred. The two stoves, the metal and the flesh one, now stood facing each other, hungering for their specific fuels. The wood stove would, naturally, want wood and coal but the flesh stove . . . what would the flesh stove burn?

"What should we burn in it?"

"Reason, logic, politeness, irony, silence."

I prevailed on Ellen to wait a bit. I asked her to leave me alone with my "Teste" stove. (The woodstove was a "Franklin.")

I wanted to commune quietly with what remained, with the new form of my spiritual mentor, with the uninsultable Monsieur Teste. If only he had acceded to my insults it wouldn't have had to end like this. It wouldn't have ended like this if he had gone back to Europe six nights ago. O why did it have to end like this? I was only a normal product of my environment. Monsieur Teste should have known that I was already an American, that his arrival had been a gamble, that he might lose. Why did he lose? O why?

In the midst of my lamentations Ellen reappeared with a good part of the HARVARD CLASSICS LIBRARY under her arm.

"See if it'll burn this," she said.

She threw the books into the "Teste" stove and dropped a match on it. The light flickered for a moment then it went out.

"We'll have to try something else."

Her eyes surveyed the room faithfully and, suddenly, her gaze fastened on our son and daughter, rolled in one, who was sleeping again. I understood her. I took its legs and she took its arms and we stuffed it into the "Teste." Not even the thought that we were on television would comfort me. I felt heart-broken. Ellen poured a good deal of lighter fluid on Maximum and lit the match. Again, after a brief flare, it went out.

"Goldarn," she said, "is there anything this blasted intellectual furnace will consume?"

"There is," I said. I crossed my arms on my chest like a soft Christ and with eyelids lowered I pointed at myself with my tongue, "Me."

"Hmmm," said Ellen. "I don't know if I want that child to grow up without a father."

*

Seventh Night

THIS NIGHT found us in profound meditation. Ellen was having a technical meditation in which the means and ways of stuffing the "Teste" stove were paramount. In her mind, she had solved the problem. She would feed the emigrant to his old ways of thinking and conquer the geography. The huge seed of the female Hitler in her began to spout technicalities.

I, for my part, was meditating on the failure of intention. I had intended, as my readers know, to inject philogyny into geography for the purpose of owning my new position. I had failed because I had relied on the coded version of my philogyny which had been Monsieur Teste.

At this point I refrained from human affairs and gave up

hope to concentrate on Ellen's motions as she slid like a suction cup toward the center of my flesh, three fingers above my belly button.

She folded me like a handkerchief and tied knots on each side of my body by tightly pulling long strips of skin slit on the dotted line. Then when I looked sufficiently like a log with bumps on it (she was no artist) she stuffed me on top of my hermaphroditic child and dropped the rest of her Coleman fluid on my shifting eyeballs. I could not see the lit match I knew adorned her fingers.

The flames licked me softly like the tongues of animals and I felt the grip of my "Teste" stove encompass and accept me as the proper fuel for its greedy form.

I burnt curiously. I burnt conversationally. This is how I burnt:

> Fuel: "It is almost like going back to Europe in a slow boat full of heretics loose on a burning sea of oil."
> Stove: "America has her reasons. She made me hungry, she made you stupid. When I am hungry I will eat anything stupid."
> Fuel: "When you've eaten me your walls will be coated with my neural information and you will lose your identity"
> Stove: "But what will happen to her?"
> Fuel: "Oh, my God, dear stove, but this is the first time I've ever heard you use the "?". It's incredible."
> Stove: "No. What is happening is that your neural neurotic nature is already coating my perceptions. There is something in you that wants to die talking."

*

I FELT ASHAMED. Monsieur Teste was returning to Europe without having accomplished his mission. I was in the air, in the form of black smoke, dialoguing endlessly with a silent partner. I had learned the final simple secret of America:

IT'S A MELTING POT. IT WILL MELT YOU.

Certainly I had not expected it to melt me in the innards of my spiritual mentor. But it had, it undoubtedly had.

My experienced friend, Monsieur Teste, was returning to his country of origin with the smoke of my mind distributed thickly on the lining of his stomach. I had learned nothing from him and he who knew everything had taught nothing.

Things were as they had been. I took my head between my palms and with a start I came to this realization:

I AM BORED IN HEAVEN. I REALLY AM. I LIVED TO SEE THE DAY.

Samba de los Agentes

MY NAME is Jose, I am Catholic and I was not a plain-clothes policeman very long. In Bogotá I wrote poetry and prayed to the Virgin every day for my mother, who was a cancerous balloon grounded in the chicken shack behind the house, and for my two sisters who tap-tapped their way past my window every hour drowned in lipstick and sperm. Here is one of my poems in translation:

> Every day is a long hallway to death
> Every night is an agony of lightning
> My heart lies in pieces at your feet
> My poor heart is a trampled field
> Bring down the rain, Mother of God

When I first came to New York I was taken under the wing of my uncle Pedro who is a cop. I fell in love with Maria who loved the Virgin as much maybe more than I did because one day, two years after I joined the force, she left me and joined the Virgin. I became a plain-clothes cop and roamed the city with two other cops, looking for crime. Because I was the first to spot the nervous, skinny

young man playing with a gun in his pocket, I was the first
to shove him into one of those doorways which in New
York stand for nature, and whisper hotly into his ear: "If
you move, I kill you." I have whispered, shouted, mumbled and stammered that line ever since I remember,
enough times to get me in trouble. It never did; I think it
is a very good line. Skinny didn't move so I slid out his gun
like a rubber from a Trojan package and it turned out to
be a toy. "What were you doing with this?"

"I was walking thinking up a poem," the man said in an
accent as foreign as my own.

"What sort of poem?" I found myself unable not to ask
although my next line should have been: "You robbed a
liquor store, punk!"

"A poem about the Virgin Mary," he said shyly, beginning to cry. I saw the tear and knew that it was the tear
said to perpetually exit from the statue of the Virgin in
Fatima. "In it . . ." he pushed on, sensing my interest, "I
was going to put my heart which is in pieces."

"What da fuck?" said one of the other cops.

Only then did I say my line: "You robbed a liquor store,
punk!" I took out the only piece of paper in his pocket, a
poem to the Virgin by A. Alien, 54 Avenue C, 2 C, New
York City, America.

"Where is your green card, punk?" I remembered my
next line.

"At home."

So I dragged him to his home, to the address plainly
written on the paper. There, we busted in the door and
found ourselves in a room wallpapered with innumerable
poems to the Virgin. The refrigerator door, which was
open, contained tens maybe hundreds of carefully washed
milk bottles, each one containing a rolled-up poem to the
Virgin. "What do you do with these?" I asked.

"Launch them to sea," he said.

I arrested him on a charge of possessing a false pistol — a
misdemeanor — and took him to jail. There, I visited him

every day until the trial because A. Alien had no money for bail. When the trial came, I couldn't be found to testify. Reached finally at the Police Academy where I was taking classes, I refused to come to court because I was on my lunch break. The case was dismissed, I was fired from the force and I became a hippie and a film maker.

＊

I WORE a bunch of dying violets in my frayed red velvet lapel. My hair is red, my hands are freckled, my eyes are narrow under long maroon lashes and my line was: "I'm from Venus, can you spare a lemon?" I weighed the lemon if I got it, raised it to my ear, rapture and anxiety alternated on my face. Suddenly I dropped to the ground, pitched the lemon high over the skyline of New York and covered my ears. When I had just hit myself with the maximum available quantity of heroin, I entered the sumptous shower of my otherwise cruddy apartment. Ah, but the shower curtain had blue angels on the clear Hoboken plastic, and the nozzle covered me with gold sparks. One eternity over, I rose to hunt lemons. If the profferer of the lemon was young, twelve to fourteen let's say, and a boy or a girl, I searched his or her smooth body for a place to launch my tongue. "A Cape Canaveral for my rocket!" I declaimed. More often than not, the case was reversed: I was the Cape, they the rocket. The boys or girls, of which there always was one behind the Hoboken angels, bathing in sparks, were movie stars. My camera never rested. The lens protruded from below my neck like the anus of a horny zebra, searching the movements of the world for formal impossibilities, joyful meetings of lay lines at prayer. (My camera was a way of eliminating parenthesis.) When my lens was broken — a furious Hoboken angel stuck a shiv through it — I framed movement with my thumb and my fuck you finger, or simply with my half-shut eyelid. Many stars were born that year as I continually begged for lemons. I went out, in a flurry of cinema and esprit-du-temps, and made the world shower lemons. I could extract a lemon from a policeman. My lemon-extracting line was never just dangling in the water: always taut, it could have made me a millionaire. As it was it merely taught me alliteration. One day I disappeared. Lemons became irrelevant. Great esthetes speak their lines and go. For them to stay around too long is to risk shrinking of the soul, something everyone but an esthete does flawlessly. "Americans have such smooth faces because they have no soul," Rupert Brooke explained. The soul is an adornment, I was an esthete. Decked in souls, I rose through the eye of my camera and went through the f-stop.

Hey man you an alien.
My pleasure.
Holy unclean fun.
The twink of a submarine's insides.

From the window at Blimpie's, possibilities of magic: the *im*possibility of ever conceiving of a time when the possibilities of magic might stand parodied. The impossibility of old self ensconced in a fiery throne throwing thunderbolts at young self dreaming of magic. The impossibility too of doing it. The availability of magic. Why regret going through the window? Everybody who went out the door is now stuck in the political traffic. I took different ways to avoid the snare of cliches. I confused them but I didn't nip them in the bud. Once I followed a nymph, her skirt barely sufficient for a place-setting at McDonald's, her silver braces and her buttocks followed by squiggly silver script and several pairs of heat buttocks. We marched together along with ten thousand demonstrators to the United Nations. Vietnamese flags were waving. A man was burning in a square. We lay down on the grass. Tear gas cannisters flew over us. She searched my flesh for fruit. I smeared her juices on my lips and eyes.

I became gradually more boring to myself until I stopped writing poems and started writing stories and everyone said you need an agent.

*

MY FIRST AGENT, Peggy, picked my up from rumors at a bar because she was new and hungry, and the only way she could be both was to turn each rumor into a person, and eat the pretzels in every bar. It had never — until that drizzly Manhattan day which is no agent — occurred to me that I needed an agent. The sort of people who had agents were the sort of people who wore suits and talked in those excruciating complete sentences I am now talking in, the kind of people who *smell* like offices. A girl I knew who worked in a brokerage house on Wall Street would not let me touch her until she "washed off" the office: still, from her bones, like smoke, the smell and even the *taste* of plastic turf and stock certificates, desk shavings and nylon rayon polyester shirts and socks, wafted violently to twist my nerves; I left her with an empty purse, after I threw up. The needle stuck in a greedy Debussy faun, the only record she had. These sort of folks need agents because they need the universe mediated.

"In America they don't burn books, they boil them," I snarled. She looked decidedly slutty, Peggy did. Miniskirt, tits that "leaped" from the leather work of a bondage artist, short, fat limbs which bespoke of a formerly round Jewish girl on a fierce diet, a blinking red cunt I could feel pursed directly at my immediately cognizant cock-eye, lipsticked X-rated red lips, all outlined by phoney cheer like a travel poster, and those pretzels, crunch, crunch. We were at a bar which used to be bearable until it filled with literary chatter like a popcorn maker. I can still hear it, a sort of low hum pierced with small press staples. Agents, of course — I didn't know it then — don't fuck. Fucking is terminal, there is nothing to be mediated. Some agents may add fucking to their ten percent but that's highway robbery so see your lawyer if you're fucking your agent. (The newspapers outside: AGENT ORANGE ON TRIAL [And don't fuck your lawyer!])

"At least they don't quick-freeze them," she returned.

The newest in death at the time was quick-freezing, a technique whereby the stiff is frozen and hammered into tiny bits then fitted into a ketchup bottle.

Peggy wanted to read my novel so I said fine why don't we go to this really fine five-dollar hotel I know and discuss it, let's just hope it doesn't rain because last time I was in there we both got soaked, and the time before that my love stiffened under me her eyes pure terror in her head as she beheld a crimson starfish on the ceiling which could only have been the brains of someone who'd put a bullet through them. An agent I figured should be able to take it. After all why would anyone shoot themselves if not for the fact that they had no agent, no one to mediate between them and the cruel cruel world.

"Here is the great work I sure hope you're up for it because it's scandalous . . . no one ever . . . no one knows . . . no one etc., etc. I wrote it in an old Ford doing 80 in the pampas and on the palisades. It's dedicated to the Virgin, the pages are stained with sex of all kinds, even sheep I did not shrink from, even a pheasant and a peacock. I had my friends hold down the neck and the feathers as I upped and outed the aviary. You understand, I'm sure, being from New York and all." I saw it quite clearly at the time. You really had to do all those things to write a novel — how else stand before Cervantes when *that* time comes? I still see it quite clearly, my first agent, a sculptured tube of lipstick, the musical slot machine paying off for all the trouble I'd gone to obtaining a peacock and a Ford and a moonlit night and all the traumas of begging for lemons. . . . I had to look through Peggy and hope that through the holey fabric of her flesh the light played as always, maybe even generalize a bit, though certainly not as much as to think that words are agents or that *I*, Sacred Mother help me, might be one too. I know now: words are not agents and I most emphatically am not one. But then, I had to work out a compromise, and in so doing I let in the ugly foot of the beast.

The hotel was out I noticed, so we shifted to a marble table in an Italian cafe, to a dark corner where I hoped to add her juices to my well travelled prose, and there, under nymphy fountains once attending to Gambino, Gallo and other dark prelates, I spread my wings of hope and begged her to love my work. Only by loving it, I explained, can you begin to fight for it, for fight you must. Above and below all such human signals — as my five fingers slipping on spilled cappuccino in anticipation of riding up your nylons — you must love and understand these words.

I then gauged her thoughts from the vantage point of what I know now, namely that she read only with an eye for signs of decay, which might be turned to profitable ends. Most certainly lost on her were the dizzying wells on whose waters luminous lemons bobbed, the peacock tropes which outshined the peacock I moonbanged, the final formulations of age-old questions on which my genius had stumbled, and the voices, all those voices I can't hear any more. I shall amend that — none of those things were lost on her — they were the very things she meant to stay away from. Like my truly eager hand responding to her falsely eager beaver, my prose responded only to her alert sense of commerce. My hand and my tropes existed only as negative signs, warnings of unsuitability. But, as I say, I didn't know agents — and she took my novel with her.

Here is the story of that novel:

Madame Rosa Alverez, the widow of a wealthy Bogotá butcher, installs herself as caretaker and mother protectress into a shabby 423-unit apartment building she now owns, and where her late husband once operated the most successful ground floor butcher shop in New York City. With the help of a young tenant — the narrator — she stumbles into a locked apartment where they make love, opening, through their gyrations, a door on the ceiling through which begins pouring the most incredible meat in the world: porterhouse steaks, sirloin tips, filet mignon, prime rib, etc., all cut to frightening perfection, utterly cold and totally fresh. Rosa and Eduardo — who are vegetarians — are buried in the animal wealth and lie there gasping for air until they rise to discover that the door in the ceiling leads into the past, namely to a place in US history called the Gold Rush. The time tunnel through which the meat travels is a converter: it converts dead Indians and murdered goldminers into fresh cuts of meat. The door promptly closes only to reopen when Rosa has her next orgasm. Brilliantly developed over a period of six centuries by the vast Columbian family of butchers — though there *are* several doctors in the fold — these meat tunnels are adjustable to any bloody period in time likely to jump with corpses. With Rosa's husband the family had begun expanding to the United States where in an incredibly short time they came to control the appetites of the natives, addicted them to the meat and took over the government. The decadent president and choice members of Congress often go visiting — courtesy of the meat tunnels — bloody periods of US history where they are drenched in the spirit of the past, Gettysburg, for instance. The meat cartel is firmly in control until Rosa's orgasm throws the operation into chaos. The Trinity which rules the tribe, namely Guzman the Executioner, Alonso the Impregnator and Juan the Guide, converges on the writhing couple covered in meat: all but Guzman the Executioner arrive on time and thus begins Rosa and Eduardo's journey to the Gold Rush where Rosa gives birth to the little girl who is her own grandmother and who will be raised by a tribe of hallucinating Indians. In the circular America described in the novel, the ecology of the world is restored because by eating their own dead ancestors Americans exit history. Very optimistic book. Title: MEAT FROM THE GOLDRUSH. 275 Pages.

A PRIME SPECIMEN of the Nixon-Mitchell architecture of the early 1970s, the Department of Justice, enfolding in its windowless interior the Immigration and Naturalization Bureau like a heart, bakes in the noon heat on the site of a former slum. The edges of the slum, like the extremities of a heart-transplant patient, lie bloated all around it, dotted with idle young blacks lying on piles of rubbish, smoking in the sun. Parts of car bodies, only the useless parts, the unsavory entrails of animals rejected by the white middle-class, rust there too, scooped up from the inside. A child probes carefully the sides of a slice of watermelon, its inside, too, scooped up long ago. The freeway, a black incision still unfinished, stands over the landscape, its wire feelers extended toward the river. The earth too is hollow, hundreds of hardhats are digging below, one day trains will rumble through. Everything hollowed out and the sides rotten — this is the world to which allegiance must be paid by the poor alien disguised in a blue leisure suit like a bad lyric in a barely hummable song — and I go forth to pay it, green card clutched tight, an official shoot within a mannered walk (I almost said manured), my shiny wingtips narrow but properly wingless, my mask in place, the eyes almost fit my glasses which I wear as prophylactics. My eyes I know without protection can make reality — or what passes for it — pregnant. A long time has flown — I have had eight watches in that time — since Jose stood at attention on the chill tar of the police plaza with a shiny badge on his tit. I watch Jose offering a quick prayer to the Virgin for his uncle Pedro who watches him proudly, his heart attack ready to claim him in five months. If I consider my twenties as a heart, the motor of my life span, I think they have been scooped violently — much in the way of a protracted heart attack — by the understanding — rapid by Columbian standards — that I have become one of the inhabitants of the underworld, a shadow in the land of the dead, i.e., an American with an agent — Peggy's heat widens the circles of sweat under my blue arms — and today I am going to claim citizenship.

The guard runs his outstretched palms alongside my body glancing at the metal detector needle which registers my keys with a slight tremor. With his palms on my hips I chuckle inwardly at the questions on the naturalization form in my breast pocket. Have you ever committed sexual perversities? Have you had any homosexual encounters? Both of these, in the affirmative, are grounds for rejection. Both of these, in the affirmative, are grounds, like coffee grounds, of my American make-up or, more properly, generational lights, beaming in their almost incomprehensible way, from a past epoch. The future, which once proceeded philosophically — which is to say inexorably — from these beams, is already in ruins, an idea junked by developments. Often, on that stretch of magnificent desolation between New York and Washington, D.C., from the window of the train, I saw the paradox of America: the future was in ruins before anyone met with it. The jumbled buildings lining the tracks exposed a complex and charred machinery that had no meaning. No one, if asked, could tell what those machines had made. Those blooms of mid-industrialization had prospered, decayed and died, without anyone's having the slightest inkling of their purpose. The future, which they had once resolutely represented, was past. The only continuity, in human terms, are these hands, resting on my hips, the beefy hands of a well-fed guard, which rest like this on the hips of a million emigrants coming here into the future: a slow dance, samba de los Americanos.

The hands of the guard became the hands, crossed on a metal desk in fluorescent white light, of the immigration officer in charge of my request for citizenship. Hands progress, in institutional neon, from resting on hips to crossing on a desk. In the bureaucracies of hands, these are the hierarchies: the fist, impacting with the face as the emigrant, stumbling off the boat, appears ready to run off the night past the guards; the index finger curled toward its owner, meaning come here, worm; the index finger pointing to the tubercular youth with two weeks' growth of beard, singling him out of line for shipping back; the vertical fist hitting the metal desk to make a point out of which, rage spent, could come forgiveness; the crossed hands, which I now face, ready to thumb through a greasy, fat file; the palms spread across the face of the man leaning wearily into them after a long day of silent hate and contempt for the Tower of Babel; the hands, finally, of the man, on the Bible, on his way up. All these hands, at no matter what stage in their office life, never lose the gesture of the guard, which they retain like a watermark.

Still crossed, the hands weigh me. Above them is the mustache of a man tensed between the incoming fat of middle age and the veneer of nearly gone muscle. They now uncross, these hands, to alert me that all has come to a point: the file. A mystery to both of us, the file is going to determine my status. My name, JOSE A., is embossed in red ink on it. The file opens. The man's eyes widen from the first page. So they know everything, I think. They know about the Virgin and the man I failed to jail because of Her. They know about the lemons and the Hoboken angels. They know about Peggy. However, I am quite certain, they don't know a thing about me.

"Why have you been driven from the force?"

"For the love of the Virgin, by Jose!"

I replace "By Jove!" with "By Jose!" to spice up the native parlance. One thing I knew: the man in front of me was my age and he had only recently become a native. I don't mean that he was a foreigner, he was as American as they come, but there had been no natives in my generation until recently. My generation — I can prove this — is the most hated generation in the history of America. Partly to deflect this hate and partly because the prematurely old young are tired of fighting, we have almost all become — over a brief span — natives. Until recently, we were all strangers and exiles, living in a place called "off the wall," which is no place. But like the tide going in, my contemporaries pulled back into the sea, leaving on the beach only the true aliens and their metaphysical brothers, the hunted. However, in beating this hasty retreat astride flying K-Mart lawn chairs, my contemporaries have also left behind the shapes and masks they had worn during the party and — this is serious — inside those shapes and masks they have left their bodies and their hearts. As the shapeless goo engulfed them, some of them noticed and screamed. But it was too late: all that wealth of brain and heart was now property of the straggling aliens, by Jose!

I regarded my interrogator calmly, assured that I had him. He was not at ease. My file was full of strange, unsettling pieces of his own past. Vague regrets coursed through him like phosphorus through protozoa. . . . Once he too had, in the dim light of an attic, been bitten by a spiritual lemon which bounced, creating spirals and cones in the air and then came to rest on the Peruvian shawl Her naked body sprawled on. He had seen the Virgin, I was sure of it.

"In 1969, you were arrested for harboring minors. What was the deposition of the case?"

"Fiction."

"We shouldn't let your past stand against you. If you tell me the truth there is no reason . . ."

"My past doesn't stand against me. It doesn't stand against you, either. My past doesn't stand at all — I am another person now. I write novels. I have an agent. I am an American."

Whatever his doubts, he did not doubt the file. "Tile is an anagram of life," he sang to himself, almost drowning, though not entirely, something else which sang, "All strains will be played out." But the file, drawn like a primitive imitation of a flower from the innards of computers, field reports, denunciations and informer asides, contained in its body, the truth and the whole truth as accurately as the science of the day was capable of it. We

were living in a time when public revulsion, in the form of
the Freedom of Information Act, had brought a rain of
files on citizens. Files and their subjects were meeting all
over America like persons and their lives on the TV show
"This Is Your Life!" For an instant, life was reduced to its
filable propositions — fallible I should say — and everybody
was able to read their obituary. What else is a file or even
a biography? A reductio ad absurdum, an obituary. A
peace descended over America, a pall, you might say. This
peace, this pall, this foretaste of doom, is repeated every
time someone opens your file. There you are: your inside
equal to your outside. Rigor mortis sets in as facts come
to life. No, there was no way my friend here could ever
suspect the truth or even that the truth might not be in the
file. He had viewed the Virgin but she had not spoken to
him.

"There is no reason, if you tell the truth, why you
should not, in time, become a citizen." He is generous with
reason. After all, it isn't *his* reason he's being generous
with. It is the reason of the founding fathers who wanted
all the orphans. However, the world is full of orphans and
he doesn't think the founding fathers meant *all* of them.
Why, a man could come here, display his orphanism, and
be allowed to shake down the lemons off the first citizen.
We must make sure he is a good orphan. Not orphan
enough that is to *cry* for love, for chrissakes, not a pathetic
fucking *ultimate* orphan . . . A reasonable orphan, a
dignified orphan, a calm orphan. Jose A. here is quite obviously an orphic orphan, even though he's wearing that
ridiculous suit. You can smell a new suit an elevator away.
Like all high-ranking civil servants, he lived under the
building. He rose to work in an elevator and descended
home in a paper cone. A cardboard vase filled with paper
roses awaited him: his wife. She bobbed her many heads,
and hamburgers came out. The evenly spaced skis along
the wall invited his feet to strap in and go: his children.

"Your file raises questions."

I too raise questions, darling little things, on the window sill of my cruddy apartment smoothly run by Madame Rosa Alvarez. "We will look into them. I see no reason, etc., if one day etc., if the truth, etc., you may not, etc., one day, etc."

*

YOU CAN GO quite far on a word. The word "go" for instance. An insight like that can go a long way — possibly the whole way — toward making an agent. Agents are born from aphorisms the way other people come from mothers and fathers. That insight has nothing to do with the agent — it is an insight about writers. Properly, a writer can go quite far on a word, the word "go" for instance. An agent is the creation of a random aphorism about writers, then, and think how far a writer can go on *two* words: "go, man," for instance. "Man" is an addition of genius — it is the agent's coming of age. The aphorism slanged. The insight humanized. The inserted concern. The bridge. Go, girl.

When I hadn't heard from Peggy in a year I got tired of leaving words on her tape machine and staked out her building. She came home with a young businessman with a bushy mustache in which cocaine flakes were embedded — I could see them from the fire escape. Under a low-cut glass table on artificial turf was my manuscript scattered, open, and I could see the page where the narrator discovered that he didn't remember anything he wrote, and that by rereading what he wrote he could predict the future. His writing, he decided, was oracular and on that page he revealed his methodology.

"What do you do?" the businessman demanded of Peggy, now that a slight burning sensation seemed to attend his still-tingling nub. He could well imagine his wife receiving penicillin.

"I am a masseuse," Peggy confirmed. "I just wrote a book." She pointed to my manuscript. "I describe my life in there for a million dollars which I am going to get as soon as Xaviera Hollander writes the blurb."

When he left, my agent chuckled to herself and still in bra and no panties began to play with herself right in front of my face in the window which she suddenly saw. I pulled up the window and went in.

"Don't move or I'll kill you," I quoted myself.

I killed her.

I did it as I had been taught in the police academy, two squeezes and a chop to the back of the neck. No mess. I then fed her half-dead cat and watered the totally dead cactus and then turned on the tape machine with her messages.

"Hi, I hate to talk to machines. This is George, the author of THE VATICAN FOLLIES. My parish priest says he knows a publisher."

"Hi, this is Dr. Lupus. I have a superb idea. It seems to me that people have been turning into rocks. Over the past ten years we have been slowly petrifying. 'Petrification,' the O.E.D. tells us, is the gradual numbing and hardening of the cells. At the rate of present day petrification, it takes ten days to turn into a boulder. The eyes become shiny, reflexive pebbles turned inward, rolling in their sockets like marbles. Just take a walk, see for yourself. We could turn this into a slab of a book, with examples from contemporary poetry and pictures of rocks. That will do it. Damn it — denying me tenure after fifteen fucking years . . ."

"Hello. You don't know me. I'm a mangled dude who decided to turn his suffering into a book about my experiences. But I'm mostly a victim of the sentence because I can't write one. If you get me written I'll give you all the money."

"Hi, baby. I'm a gambler on the big time gambol. I have a system now that's one hundred percent. If you can get me ten Gs I can make you, your mother, the publisher and all the suckers who read, real rich. Do you think a gambler's desire is money? Wrong. It isn't. A gambler's a mystic — all he wants is total attention, total presence. At that table there is no one between his concentration and himself. Money's nothing. Beats yoga anyday. We could sell it as a spiritual sort of book for people with money who can't sit still. A gambler don't need an agent, baby. I just need money."

"Peggy darling, where have you been? I'm worried sick about this business you're in: your father got it into his head to move onto a barge in the Hudson . . . you've got to talk to him, dear, I get seasick so easily. . ."

Peggy had been the consummate agent. All this had interested her, all the unfocused fantasy of America had channelled through her like toxic wastes through the Love Canal. She had seen herself as a purifier, an air filter, a meter gauge on her country's demented psyche and that's why she had been horny all the time.

*

WHEN I CAME HOME Madame Rosa Alvarez had a surprise for me: she flung open the door to my crusty rooms and there, in a circle reminiscent of a village dance, all embroidery, high-heeled shoes and black and red hair, were my mother and two sisters. The result of a miracle still much discussed in Bogotá, my mother had deflated and her cancers had been sucked out of her. The renowned psychic surgeon Xavier Urmuz had had his picture in many papers as a result, particularly the dramatic one which shows him stepping on wriggling brown spots pouring out of mama's body like hailstones through a grass roof.

My mama became a rapid American. So rapid I took her to Atlantic City, and for a moment there I panicked, I thought I'd lost her. Looking over the dazzling rows of madly whirring bright slot machines, each one facing a wrinkled middle-aged woman in electric green pants, I couldn't tell which one she was. It was a movement that gave her away, a jerky spasmodic upward twitch of greed, which made it seem as if she was pulling the machine off its black stem. Cherries and apples whirled past, and out of the tumbling fruit, something of mother appeared. Getting closer I noticed the fierce and familiar pursing of her lips in what was her unique and ancient quarrel with fate, or luck as she sometimes called it. Luck, luck ran through her lips in a flow of mixed syllables in various dialects. Some have luck, some have all the rotten luck. She had already forgotten her miraculous cure when faced with the evidence of her machine-neighbor, her identical image, her fellow bus passenger, pulling showers of silver out of the air. Before the coin she proffered to the secret quarrel with her destiny had even reached the insides of the machine, she pulled it hard and stalled it. She had to duplicate her movement every time, as the arm of the one-armed bandit would not comply the first time around. This double-movement, notwithstanding the miracle, running as it did through her whole life, divided her days and nights. Her days were now dedicated to achieving the semblance of an American woman. She competed for blandness in endless shopping sprees, which were fast draining my sisters' hard-earned whoring money, and which yielded the same plastic colors as the stuck slot machine. Her nights were occupied by the dead. Useless to resist, unresponsive to medication, contemptous of doctors, the dead came to her every night to converse, ask and answer questions, as much at home in her dreams as they had ever been. Her years in the chicken shack had been crowded with dead people, her shack had been the coffee house of the necropolis. They had all come with her to America now, happy like all new emigrants, a dream come true. For the past two weeks, I had been sleeping elsewhere, unable to listen to the wild cacophony of my mother's dreams. My sisters, who were used to it, said that it was this constant dead talk which had driven them from home at night in Bogotá. By the time they had had her removed to the chicken shack it was too late: they liked what they did. For the past two weeks, my mother had been teaching her dead English until dawn. When the last of her quarters brought forth a mixed bag of grapes and cherries, she turned to me and sighed with the satisfaction that I, at least, looked exactly like everyone else, an investment which she had made earlier and which had, unlike the *pure* operations of luck, paid off. She had no way of knowing that the blue suit of which she was so proud — she had sent it to me by boat — had only been worn once before, when I had gone in to ask for citizenship. In her mind I was always clad in the blue suit, and when I wasn't she didn't see me. Invisible in my childhood, I was still partly invisible. Unfortunately, I *was* partly visible. This is the part that writes prose.

*

I MADE small talk with the man ahead of me, Number 15, on the bench at the Immigration and Naturalization Bureau. He was Romanian. He told me, that contrary to popular belief, Dracula was a man of the people. He was man enough to impale them. He boiled people. He stuck a lid with holes for heads over the cauldron people were boiling in. He ate in front of the boiling cauldron with relatives of the boiled. He nailed people's hats to their heads if they didn't remove them fast enough. He made dishonest merchants swallow their money. He nailed thieves to one another and impaled them horizontally on the dotted line. He poured poison into people's ears. He saved Christianity from the Turks. He invented nationalism. His portrait hangs in classrooms all over the country. He has been maligned. Then his number, Number 15, was called, and I was next.

"We have perused your file, Jose. We have half-looked into your soul and found some good things. We know that you are a writer. What have you written, Jose?"

"A Guide to Fucking in the Great Cathedrals. A Guide to Gargoyles in Ten Great Cities. A Spiritual Guide to Gambling. A Transylvanian in Disneyland."

"How do you make a living?"

"I am a philosophical fashion arbiter. I decide what colors the ideas should wear."

"Do you make enough to eat?"

"Enough for Shrimp Imbecile for two. Sizzling flied lice too. Flied polk! Oystels! Egglolls! Watel! Evelything! I am a well-fed American who doesn't even moan in his sleep . . . though the silence was terrifying at first."

"I sense a bit of resentment. An old wound, perhaps?"

"Yes. The wound winds all the way around my body, through the air. My aura is unzipped. A kind of spare lyricism attends my movements. Sometimes I am Spartan and hemophiliac at the same time."

"That sounds like a paradox."

"To find a true paradox you must dig at least six feet. I sense nothing of the sort. True, I have had many serious, late-night discussions with people in the know. The world is dying."

Getting up from his desk, the immigration agent looked furtively around then closed the door. He winked. I understood from his automatically lowered voice that his inner police ear had been activated. He implored me to listen to his position. He spoke cautiously, as if behind every word someone or something waited for him with a slingshot. He tested each word in his mouth, prodding each letter with his tongue. Even to himself he appeared as a conscientious consumer, making sure of each tomato before buying. But his words, when finally released, turned over and bought, came out tired, boring and insipid, settling on me in their reasoned predictability like flies on the summer sweat of a bald pate. I have no idea what he said.

"What do you mean?" I asked.

"I can't tell you that. Suffice it to say that under the

circumstances, we will have to keep working on your file until every shadow of doubt is erased. The whole world comes through this door: Vietnamese peasants, Cambodian spies, Cuban killers, and writers. You know . . . I have here something a writer once wrote, I flushed it out. . ." He handed me a dog-eared mimeograph pamphlet entitled DIALECTIC OF TERRORISM, OR THE PLEASURES OF EXILE. Leafing through it I saw underlined: *Rely on your basic transparencies.* On the margin, a hand had scrawled: *Pictorial key to terrorism.* I saw also *Happiness is a loss of integrity*, and on the margin: *Psychological milieu.* On the back cover was a picture which looked like random meat after a TNT blast: the caption said: *Fragments of a Comrade.* "Needless to say, we had the author deported. . ."

"Why?"

"Anarchism. Subversive milieu."

"I have arthritis of the milieu," I confessed.

"On the other hand," he continued without hearing me, "we have a writer who deserves to stay, it is a pleasure to keep him." He handed me a poem.

COUNTERREVOLUTIONARY SONG SUNG BY THE WHITE GUARDS IN THE UKRAINE 1921 IN PRAISE OF THE UNITED STATES – A NEW TRANSLATION BY (name deleted)

At the small arms seminar
Vera and I whispered about Lenin's bananski
There isn't any said Vera
He left it behind in Indianski

The mountains are covered with manna
We have only just begun to fight
Like the corn in far away Indiana
We will conquer the Bolshevik blight

At the small arms seminar
Aliosha inserted the firing clip for Anna
A snow drift came from the mountains
As beautiful as the hair of Fata Morgana

We will stomp each Bolshevik with our boot
Like a wiggling scarlet piranha
The mountains will be free forsooth
And we will be famous in far away Indiana

I handed it back.

"You know," said the agent, carefully folding it in four and putting it back in his suit pocket, "to this day the Cossacks are very famous in Indiana. In my little town we have the Cossack Inn, a White Tower and we have a corn ritual where we sing Cossack songs."

"How long, then?"

"No one knows. Form's just benign content, as the doctors say . . ." he said, waving my application, "but content may well be malignant form . . ." He pounded my file.

*

I HAVE a new agent now. He wants me to be a ghost. He's on to something; if he can turn America's hungry writers into ghosts he can turn the ghosts into cash. And when you see the creations of ghosts on television, conjuring their ghosted memoirs amid the snow and the ghosts, you think, why not a ghost, everybody's dead.

Things knot though when the ghost I am to be is ghost to the first lady of forensic pathology. "In his life time," she says of her late, beloved husband, "he has carved up 37,000 corpses." All those ghosts, I am sure, are all eyes and ears as the marvelous scientist incises their former eyes and ears. "Ah," they say, "What wonderful fingers! What a splendid wife! What charming children! What parties! What friends! What fire! What objectivity! What courtroom manner! What honors! What a life!" They should know, they are all his ghosts, part of the doc's own TV show: ALL MY GHOSTS. In his life, the famous pathologist caught criminals like flies. It was his splendid embalming which brought to light the heinous murder of an acrobat by his lover, a circus clown: exhumed two years later, a trace of the poison was still preserved in a needle track in the creature's left buttock. So masterful was his analysis that years later, pathologists all over the world are still asking for slices of the acrobat's buttock in order to make independent studies. Such textbook cases!

The doc himself has now been a ghost for two years. His greatest accomplishment, a seventeen-story institute of forensic pathology, dazzles the casual viewer with the gleam of its endless stainless steel drawers, each one containing a cold corpse ready for science. In the scintillating formaldehyde chill, white-coated young doctors in the bloom of first youth move softly on pink slippers, with tinkling chrome trays or, at festive times, cocktail glasses. The institute is known for its parties — forensic specialists the world over gather here to thrill to new autopsy techniques. But the place hasn't been the same since the great man left us. This is why his beloved wife has called the ghost agent.

The ghost agent is young — he has, of course, a bushy mustache — and he hasn't been an agent for very long, only since the unfortunate and untimely demise of an older ghost agent who is now a bona fide ghost. The charmingly titled manuscript entitled HOUSEKEEPER AT THE MORGUE or LIVING AND LOVING IN THE SHADOW OF DEATH is on his desk the day he takes over the office. He pays it scant attention, he barely has time to breathe, what with all the hoopla attendant to the funeral of the older agent, and the thousands of funeral invitations, some of which haven't been sent, and the telephone ringing every few minutes with people wanting to know *who* was going to be at the funeral, and him having to explain over and over that, yes, it was well worth the party's time to attend because anybody who is anybody was going to be there. . . . But the manuscript keeps bothering him, lying there on the desk right next to the telephone, imploring mutely to be ghosted. Might as well take care of business now, he tells his girlfriend who is lying on the vinyl sofa with her feet in the air, smoking a joint and regarding him with amusement. So he calls me.

I am sitting quietly on the stairs of my building when my mother drops the telephone receiver out the window on me. I have been sleeping on the stairs at night, watching my sisters transform the neighborhood into a little corner of Bogotá, and I get all my calls here. "Do you want to be the ghost of the morgue?" he inquires. Well, I'm surprised the place has no resident ghost. It is a little like a shoe factory where none of the workers have any feet, but I'm hungry and pondering as usual my citizenship, and the only superstitions I harbor have to do with life not death. So I say, "Yeah, well, lemme mull this over, lemme think about ghosts, read up on em, maybe look at some pictures, watch some TV, study steam, listen for creaks — there's one . . . it's my mother stepping on the raisin bran — sniff this out, I'll be in touch later." Formaldehyde has a rather wonderful smell . . . I remember all sorts of horrible things in pukey old museums. What the fuck, the offer doesn't sound all that bad. So I call back and say yes, and then just like that, I'm the ghost of the morgue.

Great, my ghost agent tells his girl, he's taken the job, now I can get on with the funeral and my career.

My first ghostly duty is meeting the forensic widow, and for that purpose I shout the number to my mother who dials it three floors above my head, a telephone number you would do well to note because it is possibly the only direct line to Hades: 201-665-2341.

"I only want to know one thing, madam: was your late husband for or against ghosts? I wouldn't want to have him on my back."

"To a certain extent," replies the spirited old woman, "he must have been for them or he wouldn't have spent his life trying to vindicate them by nailing their killers. On the other hand, if you and his ghost become involved in some sort of astral skirmish, I'm on his side no matter what, do you follow me, young man? This is why I'm paying you. Has your agent discussed the contract?"

"He has not."

"Well, you're not a ghost until there is a contract. Contract . . . ghost! Get it? Ha Ha Ha!"

At the morgue where we meet, the silver grey couloirs are blazing with light. Neon lights are sending down beams so powerful that they develop the memories of employees like photographic plates, causing them to remember things they had never experienced. Everyone wears dark glasses and I, who do not, see halos over every head. Erect but mushy like an overgrown banana, my yellow-clad host takes my arm and we visit her hero's empire.

Floor upon floor of cadavers unfold before my rapt gaze, dancing to the measured cadence of the widow's tales. It was in this room, for instance, in tray number 625, that the good doctor extracted the sliver of the silver bullet which killed the richest heiress of the 1950s. In these four trays once lay the bodies of the four Kent State students killed by the National Guard. In this drawer was the shrivelled body of a kidnapped steel magnate. And it was here that bits and pieces from Richard Speck's Chicago nurses came to meet the eyes of the formidable doctor. "This, you might guess," she said pointing to an oversized niche in the wall, "was especially built for the five men who self-immolated in the United Nations Plaza. In there we had Jimi Hendrix and in there Malcolm X." We then arrived at the top, a recently finished room where the temperature was an eternal 16 degrees Fahrenheit. "Here," she said, "are all the unsolved crimes ot recent tame. For instance," she smiled, as a tray slid silently from the wall, revealing the beautified remains of my old acquaintance, Peggy . . . "No one knows who did it or why anyone would."

"Yes, Madam," I said.

✳

MY SISTER TABITA'S BOYFRIEND gave her the crabs and now she can't work. She's been told by everyone, myself included, to get rid of them, but she demurs. "Crabs," she says, "are jewels from Venus." She clings to them as if they were ideas. She says that at Lourdes, Christ's tears fall on his toes and turn to gelatin and then his greenish fungoid feet, soft and wobbly, walk over the minds of his worshippers. "Would you remove his tires?" she screams. "I am no less attached to the ancient rottenness of my whimsy!" she hollers. I try to talk sense into her. "If Christ would think of us as fondly as you think of your crabs, Tabita, we would all be in Heaven!"

But there is no talking to Tabita and now there are crabs everywhere: in my hair, in my eyelids, under my arms. I didn't even sleep there — I got them just by sitting down. And as I get up, I can't make up my mind if the little beasts have colonized or inhabited me. Likewise, our earth must at times ponder this question. I know it is not an appropriate moment, at the very beginning, nay, before the second chapter of THE QUEEN OF THE MORGUE (as I retitled my ghost job), to ponder this, but nevertheless: when writing, am I colonizing or inhabiting the language? Until Peggy, I would have laughed this question off as utterly stupid. Until then I had been sure that words came to inhabit me, little astral spores in search of a mouth. Shortly after I thought, well, perhaps I am inhabiting them, though Lord knows *what* inhabits them if that's the case. As bad as that proposition was, it can't compare to the criminal magnitude of colonization. And yet, as a still honest — though barely — ghost, I must ask. That this sort of inquiry is utterly inappropriate for a ghost, was made abundantly clear to me by my ghost agent, who having just read the first chapter of THE QUEEN OF THE MORGUE, tells me that my "love affair" with the American language is somewhat one-sided, as if I'd persuaded her to give me an unrelectant hand-job and then lost her phone number. There are true ways of writing a story, you little prick, even if I have to — as you never tire of pointing out — make the old bag look like Mary Queen of Scots and her ghoulish departed hubby like Sir Galahad. Ways of making it believable at the very least. Truth is like rooms one looks for in strange cities. You don't know the neighborhood, but you have to trust your idea of a room, even if it's only the fact that it's got to have walls. But try fighting conformity with your feet in the goo; the material is like a rubber tree. No one is ready for the slightest bit of truth. But don't worry, it isn't you who points the gun at my head. The hand that types is the hand that squeezes the trigger, and rocks the boat that rocks the cradle, as Tabita says when her boyfriend implores her to be normal. I must remember, in whatever twisted fashion, to allow language to breathe, ah, ah, scratch scratch.

Tabita's crabs and mama's poltergeist have turned my habitat into *Luna 4*, I can't even eat lunch there without drama. The poltergeist, a recent escapee from her nightly cafe for the dead, turns chairs over. If I look away from my bowl it turns the soup into my lap. On a mild day, it's only Tabita's feather hat floating around the room and the dead flies in mother's Inca Cola swaying from side to side and the glasses in the cupboard toasting each other in an intimate sub-tinkle. I can live with that, but on bad days it breaks windows, snaps legs off chairs, breaks mirrors, twists doorknobs, lifts up the couch, aims knives and forks at the flesh. On days like that, interpretation wears thin, the severe diet of faulty premises begins to show itself as ribs, I see the skull under the peachy skin, I feel like Little Red Riding Hood and the Wolf all rolled in one, my face half in shadow.

Tabita's boyfriend, who plays guitar, plants his mournful physique and his untuned instrument a few steps over my sleepy head and lets go fortissimo all night of such classics as DON'T WAIT FOR THE SHRIMP BOATS HONEY I'M COMING HOME WITH THE CRABS or THE ALBINO SEXPOT BLUES which, when added to the amplified gravel of mama's soccer-crowd-sized company and the poltergeist crashing the furniture, and the wailing of New York City in heat, seriously put language on the block. And they say America is running out of energy! Bring on the Columbians! I'm having so much fun I can't remember my name. And Madam Rosa Alvarez threatens to evict us.

By contrast, the morgue is an oasis of calm. I have been given a room to write in there, a carpeted broom closet with the brooms still in it, but I can't sleep there because they fly around at night: the brooms are brand new and there is little to sweep anyway. The uniformed negroes who flit like luna moths around at night have nothing to do. The little dust balls, the wisps of etherized fluff escaping the dead disappear into thin air before anyone can lay a broom on them.

I stay until midnight, ghosting thus: "The good doctor was jogging around the fountain of alienated youth in Central Park when the future queen of the morgue spotted him." Which becomes: "I was giving my pooch Diamond his daily dose of freedom, hoping that someone might kindly relieve me of mine — I had been a widow for over five years — when I spotted the distinguished, middle-aged jogger whose perfect body might have descended from one of my reveries." Which becomes: "I had been a widow for five years but I felt no freer than Diamond, my faithful pooch, when I spotted the youthful jogger with the distinguished white hair, circling effortlessly the fountain in Central Park." Three stages: language in an increasing state of bondage. Three stages: Jose in an increasing state of citizenship. Three stages from which a pharmacology of subtlety and health may be devised by you, people of the future.

I rise to salute the custodian who is making his ten o'clock rounds to make sure that the dead are alone. In his mind, the janitors and I are part of the dead. He speaks to no one since the night when the great doctor, who was working late, summoned him to one of the drawers. "See

removed my little suede grammar thinking all the while that continuous perception is hard work, and contamination by ancestors makes the work even harder. I leafed through my sleep library in search of an orgasm suitable for an agent. But, sotto voce and for your eyes only, I must say that I have never been either a fan or an apologist for orgasm. The only orgasm I inhabited completely is the one I had in the lap of the Virgin in my parish church when I was fourteen. I didn't know what it was, which made it so much sweeter, and as it flooded me I was so rapt in prayer I thought my angel had urinated on me.

*

THE RED SQUARE in Moscow is full of people looking up expectantly to Gorbachev as he is about to speak. Suddenly, a sound, like that of a field full of grasshoppers in August, breaks the silence: a million men are pulling down their zippers at once! And another time, when the lack of meat drove everybody crazy in Russia, the crazed Russians poured across the borders into Romania and ate all the cows grazing there. And those are just some of the things that go on behind the Iron Curtain, Number 15 told me.

Number 15 was ensconced in my former bed in the middle of my apartment, tended to by my mother with wine, and by Raquel who rhythmically brushed her breasts across his chest.

"What about Dracula? And did you ever become a citizen?" I asked him.

"Dracula," he said, "was Gutenberg's son. After Gutenberg printed his Bibles he printed a book on Dracula's atrocities. This was the first mass-produced book in the world and the world's first taste of literacy. Dracula made print successful, and the vogue it has enjoyed ever since was rooted in him. The ink of that early tale about the blood he spilled is indelible. The content of cultural democracy is a horror tale. The blood he spilled issues forth from the source of the modern mind like sperm from a bull."

"I am not a citizen yet," he concludes.

Raquel had broken the house rule. Even Tabita was not allowed to bring men in, she had to work wherever the light was dim and the place deserted. Tabita is obsessive and therefore certain things are forgiven her, like her fondness for dwarves and her passion for crabs but even she does not work in front of mother. Raquel, on the other hand is a murderous fury clad in outward calm who glows like a brilliant panther when aroused. She has been known to murder and mutilate and will no doubt do it again when the moon is full. I am afraid of her because she is full of intricate canals through which flows a crimson substance which isn't blood. So instead of throwing her on her ass out the window followed by her john, which everyone tells me I must do if I hope to assert my authority, I prefer to make conversation. Authority to me is like sleep linguistics. Words in dreams, awkward flights over rooftops.

"But you must ghost Dracula's autobiography," I tell Number 15. "If direct violence is unadvisable, you would do well to sell the object of your distaste to the devil." But he is not stupid, this foreigner. He sips his wine like a fox, intent on citizenship. Dracula, who was the father of the modern state and the inventor of nationalism, stands firmly behind him, with one hand on his skull and the other on the book.

"Justice," he says, "cannot be established without terror. Ivan the Great copied Dracula. As did Machiavelli. The fatal flaw of Western democracies, the United States chief among them, was to transform Dracula from a voice of the State, which he has always been, into a private citizen with a taste for blood. You can stake an individual through the heart, bury him at the crossroads, lop his head off with an axe, transfix him with a hawthorn bough and quarter him, but there will always be another individual ready to rise and take his place, or another movie. No wonder he's bigger than Christ! Where Christ merely offers his blood like a wimpy liberal, Dracula takes it!" Number 15 became so excited he stood in bed and lifted his wine glass high over his head. My mother took her pulse compulsively and I saw large drops of blood on the ceiling. In the tiny film of light winding through the blood drops, history marched in rags, endless waves of men covered with wolf hair.

Yes, his tale had to be written, and I said so again, but mainly to recover my body which has a tendency, when excited, to rise up on a flood of adrenaline and leave me stranded among dictionaries. But Number 15 was drunk and making doleful sounds of wooden instruments. His hands — he had dropped the glass and crashed it to the floor — were drumming on the ceiling, from which protruded two boars' heads covered at the neck by tight skins; his feet were pumping two wolves' clawed feet which operated an accordion-like contraption formed partly by Raquel's bosom; and his cock was solemnly banging my sister's echoing skull.

This is when Madam Rosa Alvarez burst into the room, her flat yellow mug streaked by orange tears, her hands in the air. "Tabita is dead!" she screamed.

"She is not dead!" Number 15 screamed back at her. "She has gone to marry the sun! The moon and the stars will be her bridesmaids and the heavens will look on her wedding! The moon will wear a red velvet dress, and the angels of God will hold their gold mirrors to her face so she can see how beautiful she is! The angels of God are blind but their mirrors see for them! She will marry the sun, and the sun will shine on earth to tell people how happy he is with his bride! On beautiful summer days you will be able to see her sitting beside her husband, the sun, greeting you!"

"She is dead, I tell you! She has been positively identified!" shrieked Madam Rosa. But at that moment the room was flooded with light and the sun, which had been in the

clouds for the past few days, came through the crepe cur-
tains and put roses on everybody, so we all knew that the
old landlady had been lying. Tabita herself came in a few
minutes later to say that she had been stretched naked on
the roof hoping the sun would come out because she was
"white as milk and freckled as a general's map," when
Madam Rosa had burst into tears over her and ran off
screaming "I knew it! I knew it! The bugs have killed her!"
Madam Rosa shook her head adamantly and declared,
"You were dead! I saw it with my own eyes! If my husband
was still alive, God bless his soul, he would throw you all
out like rabbit bones from the stew!" She shook her head
violently from right to left, Tabita shook hers from left to
right, mama began to shake hers, Raquel shook hers and
Number 15 shook his up and down — only I, in midst of
the storm that shook the tree, kept mine still because I
needed it to think with.

*

THE FLAMING buoyant defense lawyer circles the ear —
which is the accused's most pleasing feature, often nibbled
by the acrobat he murdered — with a finger so long it sends
a 20-volt charge through the jury, and sums up the case:
"This man is guilty of no more than trying to put a little
charge and zip into his life. Is *that* a crime?" Fighting that
fresh voltage are only the quickly fading shocks — about
100 volts — of the doctor on the witness stand gripping the
wooden drawer containing a slice of the victim's buttock.
The slice prevails over the finger and, shortly after, the accused fries in the Ohio chair at some 10,000 volts, the sum
total of the shocks experienced by the ladies and gentlemen
of the jury, which is about to become "Another famous
case, involving the well-known lawyer F. P. Pearley, consumed much of the doctor's time that year . . ." When into
my broom closet, limber and jaunty, pill-boxed, mink-
furred, pulling a panther on a long gold chain, bursts the

morgue widow, younger than her wedding pictures.
"How?" I gasp.
"Lamb fetuses! Gerovital! Virgin blood!"
Fresh from Transylvania where she just spent two
weeks, the widow beams from a new body. "Dracula's castle has been turned by the Romanian government into a
youth clinic," she explains, green lightning in her eyes. "I
lay on a terrace looking up at the Carpathians as young
Gypsies shot me full of unborn baby lamb juice. The only
noise was the whirring of the huge fetus blender where five
hundred lambs fresh cut from their mothers turned into
youth paste. In the afternoon the Gypsies carried me on
their shoulders to Countess Bathory's castle over the hill.
The Countess, you may recall, was arrested in 1611 by the
Lord Palatine of Hungary and charged with the murder of
650 virgins in whose blood she bathed daily. She so
depleted the region of virgins (not to speak of the fact that
she gave virginity such a bad name, that even to this day
little girls in that region beg strangers to deflower them)
that her cousin, the Lord Palatine, had to do something.
He had the Countess walled into her bath where she lived
ten years on caked blood. It is a lovely old castle, also
restored by that shrewd little government, and there we
took our afternoon bath — some sixty of us — in blood as
fresh and virginal as the Countess could ever hope for. In
addition, five Gerovital injections every evening . . . I'm
going out of my mind, I tell you!"
The widow made as if to bite me. Her panther snarled
and I ducked. She laughed heartily. "You're too old for
me, dear. How is my hubby's courtroom career coming
along?" I read her a few passages and she approved full
steam ahead. "That's just how it was," she sighed. I sighed
too because I'd made it all up.
The widow's rejuvenation threw the morgue staff into
utter confusion. They had been expecting her to die any
day, hoping, alas, because she was always underfoot, pulling out drawers, criticizing procedure and offering opin-

ions. But her Transylvanian vacation continued to work: every day, instead of dying, she kept getting younger. Old friends she had become suddenly younger than often did not recognize her.

"Is that you, darling?" they asked, every time she appeared. At last they quit asking and simply accepted the fact that an increasingly younger woman was prowling the morgue at all hours of the day and night.

She looked about twenty-five that Friday night. I'd worked past my midnight deadline and was preparing to go down the stairs when I heard a soft noise outside. It sounded like someone slipping a razor back and forth between two pieces of felt. I went out to look and the noise moved ahead of me, up the stairs. I followed it. There was no sign of the custodian who at this time took a nap in the supply room on a pile of fresh white shrouds. I followed the noise six stories where it stopped. The sixth floor, like the rest of them, was an empty hall with drawers in the walls climbing like ladders to the ceiling in the eternal 17 degrees Fahrenheit. In the dark I heard a drawer slide out of the wall and then a muffled sound like that of a body throwing itself on a wrestling mat came from there. There was rapid breathing, an ah!, then an oh! and when I turned on my penlight I saw the widow bite the face of a cadaver in what was apparently an effort to suck out the eyeball.

"Don't move or I kill you!" I quoted myself.

I killed her. My penlight was also a knife and I stabbed her in the heart with it. I found an empty drawer and laid her in there.

"Oh, God, why me?" she asked when she saw Him.

"Is that you, dear? I didn't recognize you!" He said.

The scene had somewhat awakened me so I went back to my closet and worked some more. It seems that Winston Churchill, Somerset Maugham, and the Duke and the Duchess of Windsor, had all been converts to the lamb fetus therapy. The good doctor himself had, just before he died, recommended it to his wife. He had had a harrowing day on the stand and the lawyer's continuous efforts to discredit him had worn him out. But now as he looked fondly at his wife as she lay sprawled on a woven map of the moon, her buttocks on Mare Somniorum and Mare Tranquilitas and her left breast on Mare Nectaris, he knew that the mind was elitist — it refused sleep fully earned by the body. But sleep did finally come, and in it he realized, and then saw, that the unconscious was the unidentified caller who had left her telephone number earlier with the ambiguous message that "the dark horse" was still on sale. At the door of the pantry leading to the attic where he went to inquire after the horse, he was met by a maid who spoke with a heavy Baltic accent. "My name is Reciprocal," she said. "Your horse is in the kitchen." Which becomes: "Often, when the doctor came home tired from a particularly trying day in court, I lay on the couch telling him fairy tales (which he liked enormous- ly, particularly German ones) in a soft tone of voice, until he fell asleep."

❊

IT IS A CLICHE, I know, but within the confines of a police- man's uniform there often beats a huge, trapped moth, the tips of its wings brushing frantically against the sides of the ribcage. In my old police soul this butterfly beat so furious- ly it burst its cage, and that's how I came to beg for lemons and film. It's an old story, made complicated by the fact of police love, which is that the euphoric sadism of power can never have enough to feed itself. Policemen, like the rest of us, want boundless love, and they die for lack of it. They want to bind, be bound, beat, be beaten, piss on and be pissed on, and more than anything they want the butterfly to stop the agony of its thrashing. And like the rest of us, they eat to still the ache, and eat, and eat, spaghetti, sau- sages, egg foo yung, cheese, meat, pies, candy and bacon.

The more they eat the more insatiable they become . . . the spirit is a bottomless hole. Cops have been known to aim their service revolvers at their chest, where they imagine the head of the moth is, and then fire deliriously. Often this wild firing does no more than enlarge the hole into which they then pour redoubled portions of pasta, tomato sauce and leftover casserole, until they become so large they have to be given an official reprimand and ordered to trim down. The fat cop is a tragic creature, the victim both of a furious desire for the world and of a crazed butterfly in his chest.

I am telling you this so that you may understand the spirit in which I am teasing my immigration agent who, frozen with terror and suffering in his chair, faces me, his butterfly wild and out of control, fluttering visibly and ruffling the hair on his chest. My butterfly, freed long ago, calls and sings to his butterfly, trying to lure him out to mate. I am being cruel, nay, sinister as I improvise the prettiest canzones ever hummed and ever woven, as I dive and circle and pirouette and shoot golden pollen. Come my darling, I sing, let's make a four-winged being, enter each other until no one can feel the seam, let's be utterly crazy and demonically deliberate, let's give the space horse a whack with our wings until it shoots through time, obscurity is hateful, let's proclaim the approximate clarity of feeling, let's whip out of the sordid history of the police body into the coolness of the night, let's create on route the solid delights we can't imagine!

"Level with me, Jose! I have no time any longer for shots in the dark!" he pleads.

"Yes," I agree. "The dark is bigger than all the rifles."

"Once, I too . . . considered being an artist . . ."

"Oh . . . what happened? Did she leave you?"

"How did you know?" He is surprised, but in pain.

How did I know? Because she is written all over him, just the way she sprawled that afternoon on the Peruvian blanket with cones and spirals everywhere, ready to make him into an artist, a devotee and an ecstatic until, later that evening, she left for the jungles of the Americas with two men she found sleeping in a bus station with their heads on motel Bibles and chains around their necks. Yes, my judge of citizenship, you still reek of her, her smell is indelible, she was the only one who knew the secret of stilling the butterfly. And your idea of the kind of art you were going to make wasn't bad either. You had noticed — thanks to the vision she lent you for one week — that people made all sorts of involuntary gestures: a pat on the hair, a fingernail in the crotch, a wink, a grimace, a gentle tug at a stray hair, a knee jerk, an opening or closing of hands or buttocks, raising one shoulder or another, a tip of tongue darting out. And you conceived, in a reverie, the possibility of having these involuntary mannerisms replicated in stained glass. You saw a church rising out of the floor, composed entirely of representations of coincidental movement arranged by you in classical religious scenes: the Wedding at Cana, the Stations of the Cross. After the vision you saw, for the week she gave you, people's willed and ordinary beings were framed entirely by their unconscious gestures. You even saw, though too briefly for understanding, that a great deal of devotional faith inspired people to move in ways which they knew not.

"What sort of artist?" I asked.

"Oh . . . stained glass . . . nothing much. More of a crafts thing really."

"That makes you a foreigner. If you would like to emigrate to art I will be happy to look into what I can do to get citizenship for you," I said. "Artland has stricter entry requirements than the United States of America. To come to the U.S. you need merely a clear anti-communist conscience, proof that you always screw on top if a man and on the bottom if a woman, no aristocratic titles, not even Discount, no hidden hate of taxes and no authorship of even minor crimes like drinking hootch at fourteen, am I right? But to gain admittance to Artland, ah! You must, first of all, remain vague while the circumstances are attacking or circumstantial when vagueness does. Then you must be nobody, you must divest yourself of your person, your class and your property not to speak of your so called mind and your opinions, you must allow yourself to lapse unexpectedly into metaphorical Corinthian, let no one take you for granted, you must make sure that everyone knows, including yourself, that you are capable of perpetrating any enormity at any given time, and never under any circumstances must you finish your sentences, you must never know how a sentence will end, you must escape confinement continously. That is, you must never serve your sentence, you must brutally uneducate yourself, the world is a speech malfunction, the simplest things must be a complete mystery to you and you must approach them with the eternal idiot questions like a child bearing flowers to the enormous tractor leveling the old cemetery. You must live verifiably in the huge emptiness between possibilities and decisions, loving the former, amusing yourself with the latter, and, above all, you must always be amused. You must destroy agents, editors, censors and representatives of the state as often as possible, all dirty tricks permitted, and you must approach the universe in a militant fashion because you make it up as you breathe. Also you will allow yourself to be kidnapped by all and sundry forms of whimsy and will refuse to follow plans. You will not set foot where anybody wants you to but you must visit Plato's Republic as often as you can so that you can be thrown out of it. You must not above all believe in art or any other form of confinement, you must inspire madness, impossibility and confusion. And on the ladder of discarded negations, with a mouth full of grass, holding a lit bomb, you must climb at all times into the movies which you must trust are being shown in their entirety, any questions?"

"No," he says, "only one. Can I visit your place of residence? It is routine."

"Sure. Put your coat on, man, and let's go. My mother and sisters will be delighted. They love doctors, lawyers, engineers and the rest of the middle class. In fact, there may be some already there so you won't have to feel out of place . . ."

"No, not now. How about tomorrow?"

"Fine, but I don't think you'll get into Artland with an attitude like that. But who knows, maybe the moth will bust out . . . if properly coaxed, goodbye, goodbye."

※

WHEN I SAY that mama cleaned up . . . well, maybe you know what happened to the two girls who every morning swept up dust into the eyes of the sun. The sun turned them into the stars with the broom, up there by the Southern Cross. Well, if the sky had been in the mood he could have turned mama and my two sisters into meteorites, moon vapor and echoes, because the three of them swept all day and all night. And when they were done sweeping they tore open mama's collection of liquid, gaseous and solid cleansers, everything advertised on TV since they had come to America, boxes and boxes and bottles and bottles which until then had been piling up in pyramids behind the bed, dresser and in front of the full-color poster of the Virgin, covering up her robes and the left foot of the Holy Infant. Simultaneously, grainy blue powders foamed on the walls and liquid plumbers burrowed through the pipes. Bombs exploded causing roaches to migrate, long sorrowful lines of refugees leaving under the door crack for the neighboring apartments. The windows became transparent for the first time in memory, letting in a view of dirty windows across the street behind which startled fat nudes watched early morning television. The mattresses were beaten savagely, stains cracked and springs moaned. The floors vied with the boots of old-fashioned sergeants in reflecting our faces. The ceiling

could be read like a coloring book through hundreds of exposed layers of ancient paint. "Now if I could," mama
said, "I would like to clean up the street of all these dirty
houses, this one first of all, get rid of all these people, wash
the sidewalks, suck all the dirt out of the air and move
New York out of New York."

"Ugh, look at this!" Tabita exclaimed, pointing to the
screen of the old TV she had just finished scrubbing and
sponging, "now you can see what people are wearing!" Indeed, the game show host and his guests shone with new-
found details. Ties and shoes stood out distinctly. Tabita
touched one of her breasts fondly but exclaimed mournful-
ly: "All these freckles . . ." We were all naked because our
clothes were boiling in the kitchen, spewing clouds of
steam. Our bodies, dissimilar only in the distribution of
skin, loose like a crumpled wino bag on mama, taut and
stretched over breasts and hips on Raquel and Tabita, and
pinned niggardly to my pointed bones, were otherwise and
for all theoretical purposes, the same body, particularly in
the pubic area which was stamped by four identical
pyramids of red hair. Known as "the Amazonian forests of
First Avenue," my sisters' bushes were legendary where
such legends circulate. It would have been inhuman and
unnatural for these lush growths to contain no life and
here was the rub . . . they teemed with it. . . . Mama had
tried to pour a bottle of A-200 on Tabita while she slept
but she'd awakened screaming genocide and hadn't calmed
down yet. "You might as well kill me too . . ." she
repeated every five minutes. Raquel tried to talk sense into
her: "They are just like roaches, only smaller . . . you
don't seem to speak up for roaches, do you . . . No one
else is either . . ." "That's tough!" screamed Tabita. "I
can't champion all the bugs in the world!" I saw her point:
the roaches had no apologist, no house critic, but they
could take care of themselves. The crabs needed Tabita the
way corporate publishing needs *The New York Times
Book Review*. The only concession we were able to extract

from her was a solemn promise that she would not scratch herself during the immigration agent's visit. I don't think a visit by the Pope would have caused such a promise from her. Only Immigration had such power and I never understood why until later events revealed that Raquel was in love with Number 15 and Number 15 had twice attempted suicide when denied citizenship, and Tabita loved Raquel more than anyone else in the world. Our household was a household of love and one person's beloved crabs were the others' beloved crabs no matter what we happened to think of them. And that is how it came to pass that amid the shining cleanliness, an oasis of purity in the heart of New York, only a few crabs, the more visible for being the sole survivors of a truly American cleaning binge, made their accustomed rounds in the forests of our beings.

But just when it appeared that all was in order and in pristine readiness for the visit, tragedy struck. The lush use of Lysol, bleaches, Clorox, detergents and soaps in the water, destroyed our clothes. Every last piece of cloth had boiled irretrievably away and there wasn't another garment in the apartment. The water in the cauldron had turned into purple paste. My blue suit had merged with my sisters' lingerie and my mothers' polyesters had merged with our Columbian flannels.

Only four hours remained until the visit, a time mother had deemed sufficient for the clothes to dry, but now we were in trouble. Raquel picked up the telephone to call Number 15 to ask him to purchase anything he could find but the telephone was dead. It seemed that in scrubbing the walls Tabita had dislodged the connections. Either that or one of the powerful detergents had corroded the apparatus. There was only one thing to do and that was for me to wrap myself in the plastic shower curtain with the Hoboken angels on it and go to the store, and this I did.

Roaming the streets in transparent plastic, o bards, is no big deal in our city. I noticed many hundreds of people in similar attire. I had never seen them before which confirms my law of New York which is that you only see your own sort of humans in our great city, depending on the speed of your walking and the demands of your eyes. Rapid businessmen with swinging briefcases see only their own kind. Parallel to them but slower is another world and parallel to that is a yet slower one until you arrive at the motionless bums who see only the motionless. And parallel to the worlds of speed are the worlds of tweed, cotton and plastic likewise aware only of each other. So it was no surprise really to see thousands of Hoboken angels dancing on frayed plastic around the bodies of an entire social subclass. But when I got to Orchard Street where all the affordable clothes are I saw that I had no money. In our haste to boil our clothes we had boiled away our wallets and purses also.

One thing to do then. I walked into the crowded offices of the Manhattan Chemical Bank and stood in line. When my turn came I advanced on the teller, a spry Puerto-Rican blonde standing on twenty-inch platforms, and said, "Lean over the counter as far as you can and look down. You will see a weapon pointed at you! Take all the money in the drawers and put them in a blue deposit bag or these are the last words you hear!" To make my weapon as visible as possible I filled my mind with the curves and buttocks of my filming days. I bent in memory over the deliciously spread body of the adrenaline-filled love of my Buddhist burning days, and then lowered myself into the ghost agent's girlfriend while Peggy studied us playing in the window, and helped these images with my hand, up and down. The teller leaned far over the counter and looked down and saw the weapon grinning at her and pointing straight at her ruby-lipsticked heart-shaped mouth. "All right," she mumbled, and filled a bag with cash.

Loaded with clothes and feeling not a little crinkly and quite a bit squeaky in my brand-new striped green suit and tight wingtips I flew up the stairs of our apartment, con-

vinced that a rush of bank robberies by penis awaited our
mimetic city in the next few days as soon as the Daily
News hit the stands. I had purchased lush silks and expensive shoes and exotic perfumes and Persian rugs. I opened
the door, dropped the huge parcels and saw that I was too
late.

Sitting stiffly in the better of my two wooden chairs, was
the immigration agent, his eyes riveted to the square tips
of his shoes, which slipped on the waxed floor back and
forth, while facing him, on our other chair, was my naked
mama, making conversation. On the bed, with their legs
crossed, and their arms around each other, my two little
nude sisters smiled large fixed smiles like birds about to attack a ripe plum tree.

"Yes, you should have seen my little son in Bogotá.
Always praying to the Virgin, always reading . . . Reading
and praying, he was an angel he really was . . . Would you
like to see some pictures?" Mother got up and removed
from a trunk the carefully dusted photo album, exposing,
as she bent over, her ancient wobbly buttocks atop her jig-
gling old thighs.

"If he becomes a citizen," Raquel explained, "then he
can get far more work as a ghost because no one trusts a
foreign ghost, they think a foreign ghost pulls back to the
place where he was born."

"And maybe then we can be citizens too!" shouted
Tabita, who had a problem adjusting her voice controls.

"Would you . . . like that?" coughed the agent, avoiding
but seeing nevertheless the immense brown aureolas of
Tabita's breasts.

"Here he is at ten, in our parish church . . ." Mother
moved her chair closer to him so he could look. She put
part of the album on his knees while another part rested
on hers. "Here he is with the statue of the Mountain Virgin
of the Eight Miracles when she came through our town.
Little Joselito didn't sleep for many nights before she came.
He prayed and cried until his eyes were red . . ." Page by

page, the devoted little boy went on his knees from icon to icon and statue to statue, crying rivers of tears.

"I brought you some clothes," I offered, directing their attention to my bundles. "I hope I got the right sizes . . ."

"Ah!" said the agent, "I'm glad to see *you*! Your mother and sisters were kind enough to entertain me but it is you I have business with. Could we go into another room?"

"I am sorry, there is no other room. We could sit outside on the steps . . ."

"No, that's fine. We can sit here I suppose, if your family doesn't mind . . ."

"No, no," they all hastened to reassure him, moving off the chair and beds to examine my purchases. They tore open the packages and a storm of underwear, skirts and blouses broke over the room as they lifted their legs and their arms to slip them on, and bent and shook to adjust them. There was a rush to the mirror and Raquel and Tabita had their usual mirror fight. "There is only room in the mirror for one of us!" "Mirror, mirror on the wall, who's the biggest slut of them all?" "I'm surprised you don't keep your mirror in your pussy! Then you could see yourself from the inside!" "I've got a mirror in my ass why don't you look at yourself in there!" "Every time you look in there you grow warts on your lip!" and so on, but just before they were about to let fly at each other they smiled and embraced and, amazingly, they both fit in the mirror and there was even room for mother.

"You have an understanding family," said the agent. "We place great value on harmonious family life. The family is the base of our way of life!"

"Yes, I have been blessed that way. I am lucky, I really am."

"I like your mother very much. She is a fine lady," he said, but what he meant was he liked Tabita very much because his eyes were glued to her.

At this point, the door burst open and Number 15 rushed in, one of his arms in a sling and the wrist bandaged. "You!" he exclaimed, when he saw the agent. "I almost died because of you! Where is my citizenship?" He took a menacing step, holding up his wounded arm. "Regulations . . . Forms . . . It isn't up to me . . . Procedure . . . " He was visibly alarmed. "We never determined how you came to this country . . . Where is your green card?"

"I told you how I came. I flew, that's how. I lost my green card in a parking lot in Hollywood! What more do you want from me?"

"There was no record of your flight!"

"Of all the nerve! Every bird between here and the Black Sea can vouch for me! I even smiled at the stewardesses on a transatlantic Pan Am jet and they waved at me! Jerk!"

The agent stood as if to leave.

"No you don't," grinned Number 15, a large blackened and calloused paw on the official's shoulder. "Not until I tell you what we do to tax collectors in Transylvania."

In Transylvania a tax-collector was lacerated bit by bit, until his reason was destroyed. Often, he was attached to a chair or a bed hung from a horizontal arm attached to a pillar in the middle of a dump dungeon or cave: by means of a system of gears the machine was set for any degree of speed. The rotatory machine gained speed slowly until it looked hell-driven and the sufferer's pockets shook loose all the pillaged taxes while his reason fell away in spasmodic chunks. The inventor of the rack, a Transylvanian nobleman named Baron von Bruckenthal, refined this machine to such heights of perfectability that in 1731 an imperial tax collector was completely dismembered by the centrifugal force and pieces of him were found as far as Vienna sticking in the weather vanes of some of the finer houses on Elisabethstrasse. Later, it seems, new techniques came into use, including the infamous "tax collector music machine" which was inserted into the body through what was called "a rigorous system of organic and moral penetration." It consisted of tiny disks resembling

roll music for the player piano which were put inside the
intestines, the brain and the spine. Seven strong fellows
with wooden hammers hit the wooden keys of the machine
a little distance from the tax collector who then began to
fill up with music and to hum and reverberate louder and
louder until all his internal organs started dancing. The
music eventually attained such strength that all the whirl-
ing and waltzing organs exploded, merging inside the man
in a furious and indistinct sea which rose in a single wave
and lifted the body into the clouds, pulling him off the
disks. "And that!" shrieked Number 15, "is only part of
the story!"

There was only one way to anesthetize Number 15 so he
wouldn't harm my fragile link to citizenship, and Raquel
took it. She dropped one of her large breasts into her
palms where it fell with a heavy plop and she introduced
the nipple into Number 15's angry mouth which closed
immediately and began to make baby noises. "There,
there," she said, patting him on the rough black brillo pad
most Romanians seem to wear on their heads, "There,
there," and he closed his eyes and fell asleep.

When the agent saw he was out of danger he became in-
dignant: "That man!" he grunted. "To every simple question
I asked him he replied with riddles! Fairy tales! Vampire
bats! I said 'Have you ever been arrested?' and he gave me
the history of his twelve cousins' cardiac arrests! He probably doesn't have any cousins! He doesn't even have a
mother I'm sure of that! He's a down-and-out orphan with
a big mouth!" The agent half stood, shaking his finger,
while Tabita nodded gravely, agreeing with every word.
He now addressed himself entirely to her: "Some people
think we are robots! They have no respect at all for what
we represent! And then they want to be citizens! Sometimes I think I'm being punished with this job for sins from
another life but of course I don't believe in that nonsense!
Believe me, after a day of the strangest gibberish in one
thousand different accents, I'm ready to hang my hat!"

"Hang it! Hang it!" cried Tabita, falling into his arms,
"Hang it on me!"

He had no hat to hang but he held on to her as they both
fell on the floor and wriggled there utterly penetrated, he
by red-haired Columbian heat and she by compassion and
a big man. I prayed Number 15 wouldn't wake up and he
didn't. Mama got up to fix some snacks because she knew
they would be mighty hungry when they got up off the
floor. I was rather hungry myself — emotions render me
famished — and I rocked back and forth on my heels,
abandoning myself to the familiar and lovely sounds of my
now wordless household, Number 15's snores alternating
with the content suckling sounds of his lips, the agent's
and Tabita's ahs, ohs, madres, dios, god, oh my gods, oh
fucks and the sizzling heavenly aromas of frying hot peppers, thin slices of marinated beef, bubbling beef bones
and fresh bread coming out of mama's pans and oven. Ah,
yes, even everloud New York appeared to have been stilled
outside the window in hot afternoon sun. All was peaceful, quiet and safe. Sometimes, not often enough, the
world is like this, gently immobile in an eternal Sunday
afternoon. We stop our banging and clanging for long
enough to taste the sweetness of things at ease, their hard
edges softened, harshness gone or out of focus, something
dimly remembered flows sluggishly through the body. A
gaucho, asleep on his horse, stands still in the Sierras.
There is no wind, the animals sleep. On the half-eaten
head of a cow the flies stop buzzing. The maggots too take
time off for a nap, stretched lazily in dark tunnels of food.
Sudden peace illuminates the eyes of the man dying in the
house next door. He falls into it like a fat snowflake on a
white field. I am six years old and I am watching him, not
moving. Later, when the adults come back, I tell them how
the Virgin came in softly and took his soul with her. They
too can feel the peace. This peace is a gift — you cannot
buy it and nowadays to people my age it comes only rarely. Only violence can at times bring it up, often with death

in tow. And there are many to whom it never comes. It never comes to dreamers who have become cops. To writers who have become agents. To lemon lovers who now sell houses. The price for re-entry into the society which hated them is half the hate, which they must take into themselves to lighten society's burden. A true Sunday afternoon comes only to those able to make their experience public and this they are forbidden to do by the self-hate with which they bought their way back in. The prodigal son is an anomaly, he fits nowhere, he has denied his past but has no taste for the present. His parents do not want him now, they want him then. The labor market will only take him grudgingly and then at a substandard wage, he suffers all the agonies of a turncoat and none of the pleasures of forgiveness except money and money is garbage so the only place short of death which he has also forsaken in favor of old age is Tabita's pussy and in it he goes, up and around, up and up, up and out, unaware that myriad-legged swarms of Venusian jewels are migrating onto his body, riders of the storm awakened by heat. The content of his revelation, the fleeting beginning of his abandoned art return briefly in orgasm without the mushy edges of political hysteria and they are public for the first time in his life because I am watching carefully and mama too, her pan full of sizzling red peppers held in suspension briefly, because this is one of the few moments that bear watching, being both incomprehensible and totally true. But we aren't newspapers, of course.

Number 15 woke up feeling mythological, throwing his startled body out of sleep with a stream of curses invoking fabulous beasts. He was about to strangle the agent, who was struggling to his feet when mama served the food. We ate it and with each dish we became sadder. Number 15 remembered the food of his country and began in low monotone to recite the names of all the dishes of yore. It was a litany of the dishes of Transylvania, as beautiful as a funeral dirge. And it seems that indeed, at funerals, the people of that country recite the names of all their best dishes over the body of the departed, in order to remind the angel of death that the deceased is on a special diet and will not have anything below par in the next world. Mama became sad because the peppers and tomatoes were not the way she remembered them — they tasted limp and airless, not at all like the robust vegetables of Columbia. Raquel was sad because every time she ate she got a little fatter and one day would come when she would be too fat for love. Tabita was sad because in reaching inside the agent she had found only a terrifying and whistling emptiness and now she wasn't hungry. And I was sad because the world is sad and my loved ones were very sad but my sadness was happy like rain in the fall. I was sweetly sad and not at all unhappy. The agent, of course, was sad because he didn't know what he wanted from these people, and worse he didn't know who he was anymore, and the food was foreign and it didn't warm him.

The agent left with his report unwritten — the first time it had ever happened. He strolled aimlessly through the river front park. At one point he felt what he took to be a prick of his conscience but it was only an itch in his chest hair. Soon came another false prick of conscience which again was only an itch below his abdomen. As the pricks began to multiply, he thought, well, maybe it is my conscience. After all, I was derelict of duty. Soon his entire hairy body seemed to be on fire and the passersby slowed down to take a long look at the madly scratching bureaucrat set on fire by his conscience. By this time he had almost ceased looking human as he leaped and jumped like a shaman deer dancer trying to pull off his skin. He ripped his shirt and drew long bloody lines with his nails. They went up and down his body, deep and crimson like railroad tracks. Trains of maddened guilt ran on them at great speeds. His pants and shoes and socks came off next as he contorted and rolled into balls of pain attempting to tear open parts of his body he had never touched before. It was

not much later that the moth in his chest, temporarily
stilled by Tabita and by the hot peppers, began to flutter
frantically inside him. This itching from the inside awoke
in him what can only be described as the collective guilt of
world bureaucracies. The unfulfilled nationalisms and
sadistic racisms of all the buried strains in the dream of the
uniform attacked him with the fury of their incompletion.
Every new itch said "We counted on you!" and every letter
of that reproach was a line of red ants berserk in his body.
I could barely keep up with him from the distance I was
following but I knew he couldn't recognize me any more,
so I came closer.

"Don't move or I kill you," I again quoted myself.

I killed him. I pushed him into the river, but instead of
swimming he continued to roll and tear at his insides until
a long rubber object, the likes of which float only on the
East River and nowhere else, wrapped itself around his
neck and squeezed the air out of his lungs. He sank rapidly
and I knew that it had been a mercy killing.

*

Rolling Stone magazine, the magazine for rock lovers,
surveyed its readers, the rocks, demanding to know where
they had been the night of the day President Kennedy was
assassinated and all of them all the readers had been losing
their virginity at that precise point in time being deflow-
ered in cars and motels so many of them that if you lit up
the map of the United States with little red fires for all the
cherries popped it would have looked like the country was
on fire that night and the magazine concluded that the
"You Ess of A" had therefore in a single night lost its
innocence.

I would have liked to continue LIVING AND LOVING IN THE
SHADOW OF THE MORGUE but the widow's widowed panther
ate the manuscript. Left alone in the apartment where I
delivered all the fresh pages, the animal clawed its way

through everything: Steuben glass, ceramic ballerinas, gold forensic instruments, love letters, Biedermeyer furniture, Victorian fainting sofa, butcher block counter tops, several Impressionists, books, manuscripts and finally walls, emerging into the neighboring apartment, famished, wounded and streaked with blood. And there it found and fell upon the heir of Substandard Oil whom it ate in two large clean bites. The evening papers published grisly photos of the panther as it looked finally shot down by the police with dumdum bullets, and one final picture that shows a policeman pulling the head of the heir from the mouth of the beast which lay supine on the Turkestan rug. The newspapers then dealt at length with the relations of the deceased to power including a curious episode concerning the Kennedy assassination. Jim Garrison, the New Orleans district attorney who hunted conspirators in the Kennedy case, had once served the heir with a subpoena. But the heir never testified. He obtained postponements until the panther ate him.

The widow's death made my ghost agent very happy at first, with the pure happiness of agents whose clients die with all their papers in order. "If we now play our cards right we can get the whole loot . . . We split her fiftypercenter right down the middle." Her only heir was the dead panther. The agent was so tickled by the prospect he patted the lion paw of the couch. He had made the office couch in his home. The floor surrounding its pillowed hollow was littered with the wrappers of a year of meals from McDonalds. When he went dancing he went with his couch, which was carried to the dance hall by two unemployed ghosts. There, they put wheels on it, and the couch careened over the floor scattering dancers in its wake. The couch was a hit in New York where it replaced roller skates. Couch dancing spread across the land. But in the office, in its original habitat, the couch looked rather ordinary. Under Big Mac boxes were his clothes.

It gladdened me to pour cold water on the swindle. "The

panther ate the manuscript and I have no intention of re-doing it. What a panther eats is withdrawn from circula-tion. That is the ultimate review."

The wounded agent might have torn his hair but decided instead to pull the taffy of an interminable silly argument out of his body, namely that I should rewrite the story as rapidly as possible — he would feed me steak and bennies the whole time — because all that mattered now was cash. There was no widow to placate. Words are only means to an end, he proclaimed. The idea is to create a semblance of chill glamour. He was at the forefront of the movement which seeks to devalue our currency.

"Would you hurl yourself into her absence until you took shape?" I asked him.

Waxing most definitely philosophic, he said, "A means to an end is a curious proposition. The end of man is at the tip of his penis but the end of a woman is never in sight, therefore the woman is always the means. Words as means are words as woman . . ."

Ergo, I would have had to sacrifice my sisters in order to rewrite the story. I stared murderously at the man who would kill Raquel and Tabita for a fiftypercenter split down the middle. Devaluing my currency, killing my sisters, the agent took on the light by which I need to see whom I am killing. But he was a slippery bastard and possibly psychic as well because he smelled danger and dropped the subject. He thus prolonged his life momentarily.

"I have something that might interest you . . ." He said this in a hushed voice. He lowered the window although it was hot and the air-conditioner was broken. He opened the door abruptly and satisfied himself that no one was listening on the other side. "Something so . . . staggering only a true artist would be interested. In fact, the job might be suicidal . . . I don't know if I should tell you this."

I urged him on. My interest in him was proportional to the things he had to tell me. His life depended on keeping my interest. A single minute of silence could be the end of him and he knew it. So he talked on and this is what he said: "Never in my entire career as a literary agent or even before as a young apprentice to the Gutenberg Conversion Principle have I come across anything as potentially profitable or dangerous as this . . . Are you familiar with Congressman Uberstein?"

The Gutenberg Conversion Principle is the process of turning words into cash through print. Money is printed and words are printed so it stands to reason that printed words can in a maximum mimetic state, become money. The laws regarding this procedure are put forth in a pamphlet distributed exclusively to agents. The congressman had barely put down the freshly debugged — weekly — Princess phone when in came a starving man from early radical days and shot him fifty times in the head. "You are taking over my dreams," he said before he fired.

That morning Congressman Uberstein had delivered 250 pages of a manuscript to the former partner of my ghost agent, the former ghost agent, now ghost. The manuscript contained a brand new conspiracy theory on the assassination of the Kennedy brothers. The manuscript was barely in the safe and the congressman barely dead two hours when the ghost agent suffered a violent heart attack whose lack of symptoms would have delighted the chief pathologist if *he* had been alive.

"Now here is the thing," the agent went on in a voice no louder now than the murmur of a top floor water faucet. "If any similarities exist between the Kennedy and the Uberstein assassins we may be on our way to the source . . . a Manchurian candidate factory . . ."

"And what would my job be?" I asked, pretending not to know. I knew what my job would be. I know what my job is. My job would be what my job is which is to make a bee-line for the heart of American evil. I had no doubt that sooner or later, in order to become a citizen, I would have to bathe in black waters. Now that my job was about to be revealed to me in all its technical splendor, I wasn't sure I wanted it. There was still time to pack mother and sisters and go back to a dark corner of the Cathedral in Bogotá and weep at the feet of the Virgin. I could spend the rest of my life praying for the undoing of her generosity, which brought me this close to citizenship. Like everybody else however, I am helpless before fate. I am just an average Joe really, I should have been a citizen a long time ago. I didn't have to take the *ultimate* road to belonging for chrissakes.

"Your job would be to co-author the congressman's book, using alternate chapters. One chapter of Uberstein assassin tales followed by one chapter by you on Uberstein's assassin. One Kennedy story by him, one Uberstein story by you. I have the contract here . . . you will be rich."

He handed me my death warrant, and lo and behold, it was filled with small print. The agent reached for a statuette-sized black vibrator on the desk. "Don't mind me," he said, "I'll just buzz off for a while." He buzzed as I studied the document. Dentist music or humming vibrators are the only true music for the signing of pacts with the devil. Many times on the street, listening to power drills forcing their way through New York City cement, I had the inkling of shadowy presences. The devil's favorite listening music is industrial serialism.

*

THE AGENT'S NOTE:
This manuscript was delivered to my by Jose one hour before he was shot on the stairs of his house by an unknown assailant. It is obvious that together with the Uberstein manuscript this makes a most intriguing story. Should you decide to take the job and sign the contract you could write it using alternate chapters, one Kennedy death tale followed by an Uberstein death tale followed by a Jose death tale. He never did, by the way, get his citizenship. Sincerely, Your Agent.

The Herald

"HE HASN'T CALMED DOWN YET!" The Editor slapped the day's pile of sister papers. In them were his models and his enemies. The lingering fantasia of an alternative reading. Ten years ago the pile had reached the ceiling. Now the ceiling had come down and the floor had risen.

She nodded. In some ways he was a man. In the same ways she wanted to be a man. Only being a man made it easier for him to be a man in those ways. He'd already been halfway up those ways when he started being a man in those ways by simply being a man. But she had to start at the very start of those ways to be that sort of man. The start, which was also the bottom for her, was Obituaries for the Big Paper. But this was the Little Paper and her man was the editor of it. Sometimes when she despaired of being, she thought the bottom job at the Big Paper was equal to the top job at the Little Paper. When she thought that she lost sight of the pile of sister papers, and she saw the editorial attic as the little attic that it was, and the house housing the Little Paper as a little house on a provincial street in a moth-eaten town in a lost part of America, and her boyfriend, the editor, as a pimply college kid consumed by an antiquated ambition. At those times she paid sudden attention to her fingernails which she painted bright black, and to her body, which she bent in ways recommended on television, and then she took these nails and this body and offered them to the business manager of the Little Paper, who at those times seemed to her to be the authentic man. Her obituaries at those times became masterworks of precision, little prose poems bemoaning, alongside the deceased, the death of her illusions. But just when her masterful obituaries reached the point of poetic insight from which she could have soared into genuine ambiguous mortality, the Little Paper would publish a story that shook up the Big Paper. Watching the colossus tremble immediately restored her faith which, acting like Clearasil, purified her boyfriend, the editor, of his acne, and modified his dimensions to make him appear gigantic. Closely following on the footsteps of the Hulk on television, this psychic change was something she had come to expect.

"HE HASN'T CALMED DOWN YET AND THAT'S IT! I DON'T CARE WHO HE IS!" Anger was tonic. He saw her gape and felt her desire for him steam off her frayed jeans. But there was a rub, a hitch and a kink in his madness. He not only cared who the man was, but was in fact mortally afraid of this man, who made him so angry and so mortally afraid. He also knew that he had no idea who the man he so hated was, and that made him angrier and more afraid. Everything about the man pointed to huge holes in the sky, crevasses full of goopy void. The man had been introduced to him as a rare and famous creature from outer space, who had landed by mistake in his little town and, due to an improper functioning of his wings, was unable to return to the glittering world he'd left behind. As soon as the man had landed in town, he had been advised by several witnesses to the phenomenon, to take full advantage of the illustrious stray by employing him in the Little Paper. The Big Paper too had been alerted instantaneously, and was employing the lost alien as much as it could. That under these circumstances the alien would consent to also work for the Little Paper, was nothing short of miraculous. But here was the rub: While the stray seemed to fit perfectly into the Big Paper he was completely ill at ease in the Little Paper. For the Big Paper he wrote about his travels through space, his many years of wandering lost in the Universe in search of his home. But for the Little Paper he wrote exclusively about the smallness of his present habitation, the innumerable little details of miniature irritation with the lack of life on the streets and other small matters. His entire stance ran contrary to the ambitions of the Little Paper which had managed — or so he thought — to give the impression that it was only a matter of time before it too would become a Big Paper. The alien pricked the painfully enlarged balloon of the very essence of his conceit. And when the editor respectfully pointed out the damage, the alien exploded, causing a scene which in its profound meanness threatened his entire sanity. The Little Paper, the Editor had carefully explained to the man, was against slavery, servitude and servility in all its forms, and was thus the only hope the current generation had of having those principles upheld.

"Yes," the man had replied, "The Little Paper is the only hope the current generation has to have those principles upheld and to have espresso too. The Little Paper is what holds their top quality stereo speakers together with their principles. For each item purchased through the advertising in the Little Paper the Little Paper slips a little principle into the package. Streamlined to near perfection, minus a couple of kinks like me, the Little Paper has combined purchasing and upholding to a high standard. For each full-page ad there is a full page principle. Fall-In-The-Gap Jeans are covered by news of an anti-nuclear demonstration in faroff Utah. When finally planted in those jeans, the

reader's flesh has a conscience. Stereos come with pro-
posed sewers, home computers with gay rights, French
wines with Agent Orange, modular furniture with toxic
shock syndrome. The moral payoff is instantaneous and it
has the added advantage of short-circuiting the connection
of the market to the ills of society. Eventually, as in the
case of an ad for tractors followed by a story on the rape
of the Amazon, the process is circularized and the buyer
buys the product with its specific guilt attached. Your
goal, obtainable in a few years, is to match each product
to its specific regret in the time it takes the reader to get
from his home to the store. The potential is there, dear
friend, for attaching the guilt-causing reasoning to all
products directly along with the assembly instructions thus
saving time and paper. Instead of being forced to waste
their guilt-desiring organs on several sheets, your readers
will be given only the dose necessary at the time of
purchase."

In spite of himself, the Editor was curious. "And how
would you propose to bring together purchaser and product in that case?"

"In the near future," the man said solemnly, spitting a
pomegranate seed on the purple rug, "our present advertising methods will be obsolete. Unable to leave their houses
during extended air pollution alerts, the people of the
future will be watching constant parades of products going
by on wall-to-wall screens. When deciding to purchase,
our future customer will push a button and the object will
descend from the wall wrapped in its sheet of specific
moral opprobrium. The lucky buyer will then proceed to
work off the debt, spurred on by coded guilt. You will be
able to assign writers directly to products rather than
events, since the products will in any case be where the
events are and will often produce the events. This novel
and orderly way of approaching the world will produce
immediate profits. You will, for instance, follow dough-
nuts to an anti-nuclear demonstration where, stale and

soggy, they will be distributed gratis by a drug manufac-
turer. You will follow a machine gun directly to war. All
reporting until now has been done ass backwards from
event to product. You will have a chance to straighten
things out."

"What's more," exclaimed the Editor, swept off his feet,
"the time will come when we won't need writers at all . . .
The product itself in the normal process of its functioning
. . . will zap the user with a moral charge directly. A
ninety-volter straight to the cortex . . ."

He was immediately sorry for having allowed himself to
dream along those lines. Especially since the Alien finished
his thought for him: "Yeah. You might as well sell the
paper immediately and invest in voltage from the manufac-
turer. You can go straight to the brain. And one day, of
course, there will be no need for the product either. The
consumer will plug himself into the energy source and
receive as much as he's willing to work for. Invest in
sockets . . . and kill yourself," he concluded.

"Why don't you fire him if he bugs you so?" asked the
girlfriend. "After all, the sky's the limit in this business. We
can get a hundred writers for the price of this one . . ."

She loved his anger, but it was spent. Her jeans cooled.
Her thoughts returned to the obituary of a powerful man
who had died that afternoon. It was going to be a great
obituary, she decided. Crystal clear and soaring. For each
listed accomplishment she was going to inject a final note
of the irremediable. An eagle had passed. She pulled out
the black lacquer and began to do her nails.

The Old Couple

HE TOUCHED her there. He was it, she was the city and there was the bus.

"Have you noticed how the transit system is worse in towns where there is no cafe life? I propose putting espresso bars and jukeboxes on buses, to remedy both situations."

He was her equal.

He was irony, she was subjective mysticism.

"The ironist is a vampire who has sucked the blood out of her lover and fanned him with coolness, lulled him to sleep and tormented him with turbulent dreams," said Söoren.

He was stoned and she was straight.

He was there and she was after it.

Both of them were dizzy.

They were behind something, a bright object, a dictionary on fire careening through the industrial sky.

"There goes Amy Vanderbilt," he regretted. "Now how am I ever going to learn the latitude?"

He was an adept of depth and so described himself to the nun who wanted to know why, of all things, the Virtue of Prudence?

She was nun, no one, numen, to him.

To her he was fat and she advised more lines of thought whipping through his mug to restore the native intelligence that surely, must bust through porcine desire.

Thought whips redoing sensually ethereal flesh.

Compassion filled them both to about the size of a normal person. A person, that is, unused to the brain with ready receptors for history.

Various "esprits" chased each other down the virgin psychic highways of their double cerebrum Autobahn.

But only when they touched their heads together.

Apart, their heads gave each, one minute's thought to "the sad fact that . . . the confusion of two realities, one in single, the other in double quotes, was a symptom of impending insanity," transtextualized Vladimir.

In the news, at this point, liberal democrats committed mass suicide in a jungle in Guyana. It was the first recorded act of premarxist leftwing psychosis in history. One would have expected the vacuum left by the death of Stalin to be filled by excuses. But no, the "esprits" had their way here, signalling as they were willing to listen, that the final hole had been made in scientific rationalism.

He was the one expecting. She was baffled by the mangled circuitry.

"How could such a blatant ghost phosphorize in such a clean, determinist, metonymic, structural and atheistic household?" she explained.

"What do you expect in a world where the only god lovers left, aim to make anthropologist?" veered the bus driver.

"What's the last war you remember?" he asked of the man at the wheel.

"The code says be civil to your passengers. The Civil War, of course."

People's sense of history is how well they remember their wars.

Here is the last war he remembered: Having made so many sinister jokes over the years, he had been infected with a residue of terror which is, invariably, left over by successful black humor, like a coating of grease on the bottom of a well-used pan, apt to flavor the simplest snacks with a dark primal flavor. Throwing away the pan, which in this case was his brain, was clearly impossible, so he went to war instead, with the proddings of residual malevolence in even his cleanest or most sincere moments, as when viewing a baby or smelling a flower.

Wrestling with a demon, in short.

Improper balance between wit and generosity had resulted in an amount of muck sufficient for demonic animation. It was this he had last fought, preventing his poetic instinct from slipping into institutional proceeding.

He was glad he remembered this much because he couldn't, otherwise, see himself going very far with himself as a character, because he could not escape viewing himself *sub specie aeternitate,*

rolling timelessly through the city,

on a shelf full of similar monads, individual cereal packs lined shoulder to shoulder in the Safeway, various contents of eternally simultaneous conception.

She would have gladly conceded time to the nineteenth century where it belonged, if it weren't for the fact that she hated grammar and wasn't ready for religion. "Limbo is an interesting condition," she mused at the intersection of Melville and Frisby, consisting, as it does, of sheer inattention. If she were going to pay attention, she would have to become religious, and if not, she would have to put in time, as in a slot machine. Going out on a limb, in proper limbo, was a tightrope walk between an askew glance and a corresponding — hopefully or she would fall — twitch in her soul.

He said, "The future is not historical."

The youth of the country shared his opinion. They were not having children.

She had children. She believed in the future.

There were no children on the bus.

He believed in the future too. "It's my opinion and I'm sharing it."

He used to have a guaranteed neurosis in the clear opposition of his ideas, growing quite independently in his head like tomatoes in a hothouse, and his feelings and perceptions, the real weather as it were, when tomatoes might or might not grow, but as he grew, he went, more and more with the weather. The considerable health gained thereby was only occasionally interrupted by obsessive ideas, so it was a shock when one did come along, as in the aforementioned "last war he remembered," and had to be fought, as it always must, with all the superstitions in his arsenal. Unfortunately being healthy had cut down on his arsenal and the weapons remaining were either too powerful or too rusty for effective retaliation. Mythical battles fought with childhood weapons owe their clarity (as the fog clears) to memory.

She still had the immunity conferred by regular practice of superstition. She brushed her teeth with witch nipples. At the same time she was perfectly familiar with the computerized abstractions behind the images, and could wage fantastic energy war, let me tell you.

When two senior citizens were voided into the night, the driver, Vladimir, said: "Partir, c'est mourir un peu, et mourir c'est partir un peu trop."

Eh, bien, that transportation should behave this way.

"What yoga do you practice?" he asked of her.

"Overhearing. She prefers overhearing to monasticism," said the man in uniform.

"Consider this man. The breakdown of his days into shared psychic units, a consequence both of industrialization and of his own schedule, has led to the banalizing and perhaps disappearance of mythic time. But since he *is* a mythic man . . ."

"Merci, mademoiselle."

". . . he must now invent a myth for every known quantity of time. As seconds and micro-seconds, as well as the increasing sophistication of what he drives, become more and more important, his mythmaking must match his driving speed, long ago over the official limit."

The Bionic Driver offered that the task was made even more difficult by the fact that the conversational mode (outside of New York) was utterly alien to everyone. The fear of talking had spread to such extremes it was about to overtake America's primary fear which was the fear of not going to sleep.

"At ten o'clock the streets are dark. Afraid not to go to sleep, the Americans sleep. Add to that, that wit today is more terrifying than sperm, and that people would rather talk with sperm. Why, I remember, when society was voluble, we were moral."

The two of them said nothing.

We, the silent people, hold sperm to be self-evident . . .

In Reality he was a raving demon.

In reality he was a plumber.

In 'Reality' he was her.

In 'reality' he worked for her.

In "reality" his demon was her plumbing system, and he her plumber.

In "Reality" there was no one.

But just as he preferred a mask to a carefully doctored face, he preferred a face to the thought-out nothingness.

She preferred the fall turning to winter, out the window, a clear night of gentle, windy sweetness, filled with the *materia mistica* the exuberant hands of her childhood had so easily thrown into the air of other such nights.

Surprised to see the extremely personal become so subversive, he saw the narrowing shaft, the cone tunnel, the parachute. Extreme personalism is being everybody (yeah, but do you have Blue Cross?) and only women can be extreme personalists. Of himself, only his penis was personalist.

The penis is a woman.

Being here — standing on your head.

Imperious old fart, berated the bus driver, you've parlayed seven inches of schlong into twenty-five years of slavery!

Was it true?

He touched her there.

Demented wit *à face* a cemented slit.

Petra

THE MEDIUM stopped my boyfriend at the door. "She wants to see you alone," she said.

She? For three days I'd been trudging to Madame Rosa's fifth floor walk-up in Prospect Park. We'd been conversing à trois with a bizarre character named Gustav. Not only was he not a she, but he went out of his disembodied way to make a point of it. Gustav loved strategy. He'd been a Habsburg officer during the heyday of Franz Joseph, stationed in a dusty garrison in Hungary where he'd played cards and done cavalry drills, until one day, when he was called to stand guard for Archduke Ferdinand in Serbia. Leaving Sarajevo with the Duke, he remained his companion through at least three Stages. Their favorite thing for fifty years or so had been to play astral pinochle and discuss the many ways in which the Austrian Empire could have won the First World War. The Archduke was quite bitter about it, especially after he met von Metternich and the great soldier had totally agreed with his ideas about the war. Gustav's job on Stage Two had been to catch the generals and strategists of that event when they entered the astral plane, and to bring them by the scruff of their souls, so to speak, before Ferdinand for a dressing-down. But this year, to Gustav's dismay, Ferdinand had joined Stage Four, and he was left with no one capable or interested in discussing strategy, which had compelled him to that ultimate of desperate ectoplasmic acts: making conversation with embodied creatures. The florid, flower-nightshirted, pom-pom-slippered body of Madame Rosa hadn't been his first choice, but everywhere he went in the Circle of Mediums (which looks from the other side like a deep cauldron with little circles of lights in it) he found most of them taken by snarling entities in deep communication. So he plunged into the first available one like a man finding a vacant stall in an airport lavatory, and that was Madame Rosa.

I didn't exactly like Gustav. Most of the time he seemed to be speaking to Jack, anyway. Never mind the fact that it was I who paid the madame her twenty fat ones each time, and that it was I who had committed herself to foolishly writing a Sunday magazine feature on it. At times, I felt that I was watching two boys talk toy soldiers, and once I did my fingernails and went to Madame Rosa's incredible bathroom (there were *five* shrines in there, each one with a votive candle and dead flowers under oily lithographs of muscular madonnas, and hundreds of bottles of variously colored liquid labeled "luck," "money," etc; two black velvet Azteca paintings behind the shower; a *velvet* shower curtain; a shag rug of plastic black curls resembling not a sacrificed sheep but a murdered car seat; and *glued* on the toilet were *hundreds* of pictures cut from magazines, making the whole an indescribable collage and a most unsettling place for lowering one's behind, which then seemed to fit into a puzzle only God knows what it meant to spell; and on the back of the door hung large terrycloth towels with appliquéd images of the Vatican and of every pope that would fit; the toilet paper

was perfumed, lavender and had little crowns in filigree)
and when I came back, Gustav was still talking as if
nothing had occurred.

So I was rather relieved when Madame Rosa said "she,"
and told Jack to wait outside. I could barely imagine that
Gustav had decided to change sex and have a tête-à-tête
with me. Something else was going on.

"OK," said Jack, "I've waited for women before."

Madame Rosa wasn't exactly her usual self. She seemed
a little unsettled. With Gustav she had been perfectly com-
fortable. She sank at once on her enormous floating pillow
embroidered with primitive theosophy, and started talking. It was a clear, young voice. I remembered it at once.

"Petra!" I blurted.

"Long time no see, Jockey!"

"I still don't see you. But if you see me, that's enough.
How do I look?"

"Bored, tired, losing a chunk of your soul every time you
sell another stupid article."

It was Petra all right. I felt suddenly afraid. She *was*
dead then.

"I didn't know you were dead, P."

There was a pause. Madame Rosa groaned and shifted
hams.

"Well, I'm not. I'm just tripping. I'm part of an astral
corporation I formed with Armanyi. It's hard to explain."

She didn't have to. We'd both been a little in love with
Armanyi in our school days, but she had become quite
obsessed later on. She read occult meanings in his slightest
gestures. We'd fallen out over him. But Petra! How well I
remembered her, her sleepy voice. We'd met in grad school
in Chicago. Armanyi taught the course in comparative
religion. I'd begun collating the myths of the Aleuts with
those of their Siberian brothers when my roommate suddenly quit. I couldn't afford any distractions, and this
business of finding a new roommate was a distinct pain. I
didn't want a man, especially a handsome one. I meant to

avoid chatterboxes. No smokers. No airheads. I hate rock 'n' roll. I think I rejected thirty people on the phone. Then Petra called.

"Petra," I said, "if you're not dead, why do you have to bump into me this way? Couldn't you use the telephone?"

"I can't use the phone," she said in her sleepiest voice. "I can't take buses. I can't take trains. I don't have a burro. I don't know how to use a Telex."

I didn't understand. "This astral corporation you and Dr. Armanyi formed, it isn't something fiendish and debilitating, is it?"

Madame Rosa made a cackle sounding like the boingg! of a spring deeply buried in a couch. I remembered Armanyi well. He was bald and his eyes were bottomless, black, filled with India ink. I surprised him sleeping once in his office. He faced forward in his chair, with his eyes open. I passed my hand in front of his eyes, and he woke up. "I'm sorry," he said, in that charming Balkanic tobacco voice, "I have been sleeping in my clothes as if at the beach." That image had an eerie effect on me, and when I met Petra and heard her voice, the first thing I thought was: "She sleeps in her clothes as if at the beach." After she became involved with Armanyi, and she started spending little time in the apartment, her voice deepened and she started sounding sleepier and sleepier. The day before she disappeared, she looked thin and helpless, as if she was waiting on a beach for a wave to come and undress her. Cosmic. Strange. Vague outlines. But very pretty, enticing, nymphic. Oval, dark, silky, sleepy. She'd scared me.

"Petra," I asked, "where did you go when you left the house on Jarvis?"

"To Tibet," she said.

"With Armanyi?"

"Sort of. Listen, there is something I want to tell you. When I left, you were still struggling with your thesis. I knew that the only way you could finish it was if I helped you. So I gave you the idea for a second version."

"What are you saying, you semi-dead ectocreep? That you did my work for me?" I recognized in this the tenor of some of our less subtle instants of life together. "No, no," hastened the astral Petra. "Only the *idea!*" I'd written two versions of my thesis. One strictly for school, in which proper methodology was used and common myth themes were described, classified and dismissed; and another, a poetic version, expressing my bleak disgust at the present situation of native peoples below the Arctic circles. This version, called *From Russia with Love*, was about the fragmentation of spirit caused by the bristling weaponry, nuclear heads and deadly toys that now separate brother tribes from one another. Unable to scale the rotating radar dishes and blinking electronics of the Polar cap, the Eskimos and the Siberians gaze longingly at each other through quickly disappearing legends. I submitted the first to the Master's Committee, the second to a literary magazine. I got my MA and the poetic polemic was published. I was much taken with myself for it, and still am.

"Really," Petra was saying calmly, as if we were still sitting on the sunny living room floor of our young womanhood, "I didn't have anything *substantial* to do with it . . . I only saw your dilemma and cleared your mind for its own work."

But I wouldn't have it. Disembodied or no, this was the same Petra I once — in one of my moments of uncertain reason — fiercely desired one afternoon, only to be reasonably turned down. Her disembodied voice seemed suddenly full of that body, and I filled with the memory like a sail with a spring breeze. I shut my eyes tightly and rocked a little back and forth. The stab of embarrassment came as expected. It came every time I thought about it.

"What's wrong?" said Petra's sleepy, faraway voice.

I opened my eyes. "Then you can't see everything?" I said.

"I can see everything connected to a certain plane of

thought. I have little insight into desire. That was part of the deal. But I see that you are tired, that you are falling into a routine. A real danger to spiritual life. You used to be so adventurous."

I didn't remember being particularly adventurous. I'd gone to school for too long. The most adventurous thing I remember was getting drunk in a Black jazz joint on the South Side of Chicago, the day Petra had gone. She'd gone, leaving this message on the refrigerator with magnetic letters: GONE TO INDIA. I sat in that joint, having accepted the protection of a flashy dude with a gold tooth, scrambling that message in my mind, until I came up with ONE GOAT IN ID. Satisfied for the moment, I let him take me home in his pink Cadillac, and didn't answer the phone until graduation.

But she had a point. Routine was getting to me. Jack, outside the door, was an engineer, and the house was full of blueprints.

"If I go to Chicago and ring Armanyi's Tibetan bronze bell, will you be there, Petra?"

"Armanyi?" she said. "He's been dead for years."

"Then . . . you . . . why not you?" I shouted.

Madame Rosa opened her eyes. Sweat streamed down her volumes of flesh, her library of flesh, her Encyclopedia Britannica of flesh. She looked exhausted. "Wot speereet, Miz Jokey!" she groaned. "I should you pay me feeftee for dis!"

I looked at the fire-escape window painted Giotto blue. A teenager was smoking a pipe on it.

When I went out, Jack said: "I know why Gustav wanted to see you alone."

"Why?" I said.

"He wanted to propose. You always listen so patiently to him."

Julie

A BAR for the newly bearded opened on the corner. Club Moderne. *Club. Moderne.* The first is typical of the ambitions of the newly bearded: to club up, to be among their own, to club anybody strange, to be British, if possible. The second is ironic and named after the style of 1950s lawn furniture — the first mass-produced plastic — which is becoming collectible now. "Moderne" also stands for chictacky, which counteracts a little, the stuffiness of "club." In any case, the name is perfect and the newly bearded flock to it like flies.

Above analysis is the work of my girlfriend, Julie. I was studying the mysteries of the street from the window, with a cup of coffee. A bag lady was stopping traffic. A stuck clock over the newsstand said 11:32. Stupid. There isn't a clock in the vast literature of stopped clocks ever stopped at 11:32. In Russian novels they are always stuck at 3:00 P.M., which seems to be the hour when most Russians search their souls for some reason. Maybe because that's when it gets dark in the winter in Russia. In French novels, clocks stop at 6:00 A.M., an hour all the more mysterious insofar as no French man or woman has ever been awake at that time. It is the hour of children, the hour of concierges, milkmen, and guilty adulterers. The hour, in other words, when the French feel horrible. In Prague and in Czech-German novels, the big clock in the tower is always stuck on the midnight hour by the figure of Death with the scythe. For Czechs, as well as for other Eastern and Southern Europeans, midnight is political. In English novels . . .

"There is a fly in your coffee, your apron is backwards, your hair is a mess and what's with all those assistant professors across the street?" asked Julie.

I looked. Next to the entrance — tan wood with a bulging porthole — three newly bearded men stood rigidly under a street light — on in the daytime — looking pyramidal and hieratic. They formed a frieze, a moment of Graeco-Roman embarrassment. They looked as if they'd just shaken hands and felt bad about it. They looked as if they'd gone to school for an eternity and that they would continue to do so for eternity. They looked very defensive.

"Life has dealt them a mortal insult," I spoke.

Whereupon Julie analyzed the name of the club.

I could be in love with Julie, because she will say, apropos of nothing, after reading a *Time* magazine article: "The flowers had syringes." Of course, I could reconstruct her thought, retrace her path, find how a notice about Fernando Arrabal and an anti-drug poster in the subway contributed to it, but it would be useless. I would rather she went on, as she usually does: "And the flowers had frozen food, and we had the flowers. Criminal." To which I would add: "My cousin Eddie's little girl, Blue, doesn't go anywhere without flowers. Their car is full of dead flowers. The lawn is devastated." But I am not in love with Julie, I'm just not sufficiently inclined in that direction.

After a few hours, there was an ashtray full of her white-filtered Carleton butts and my yellow-filtered Camel

Lights, two cruddy cups of coffee and milk no sugar, two glasses of sweet wine and an empty bottle of same.

"Well, should we try it?"

"Let's."

I twisted my hair in an unravelling climber's rope, stabbed at my lips with a black lipstick and put on a long sweater that would do fine for top and bottom. Julie put on some Jackie O. sunglasses. Just in case, I put my diaphragm case with the yin-yang sign I painted on it one night, in my pocket, next to my Camels. We were ready for the nouveau hirsute.

I felt neon-nausea right from the start. Blinking blue signs on the other side of the bar. Expensive leather jackets. Women like labels peeled from Sunkist oranges. Mixed drinks the colors of tourist brochures. Swizzle sticks with skulls on the end. Bumping against people I couldn't help noticing the hard square of plastic set in their behinds like a little window for the cogitative dwarf inhabiting them to look out from and reflect. And I heard: "What makes it work?" "What makes it go?" "That a way to go!" to which Julie added: "What makes it fly?" and I: "What makes it float?"

It's getting easier and easier to put people in poems without them noticing a thing. I can take this fat creep right here touching my elbow and put him between the lines of a couplet, thus: *Creep*: "I coulda had it just like that," *Me*: "I ate the barracuda's cat." See if he'll ever get out of there. Caught behind the bars of that couplet, he'll be calling for mercy, but only Julie and I can let him out. I ordered another Jim Beam on the rocks, and Julie got a green green Chartreuse.

We sat there when they said: "Sit here, ladies!" Where we sat, the black leatherette was still warm, having been vacated by two rather peeved females. Like the rest of the neo-hairies, our beaus had cornsilk-in-moonlight, amethyst-in-milk, brand-new, first-time-ever beards. They rustled and trembled like virgins shaken by moonrays. The sandpaper of the underworld waiting patiently on the other side of the mirror, hadn't gotten them yet.

"According to Fourier," said Julie, "human beings should have six orgasms a day: three with friends, and three with strangers."

"We're friends," hastened the left one. "We work for Channel 4 . . ." He extended what appeared to be a friendly arm but was in reality a dead stick of petrified wood from a California petrified forest. Like many other young professionals he had not enough life in him to reach through all his extensions. There was barely enough life for the beard and part of the lower lip. The rest of him was without gloss, mostly petrified, and some dead wood. The limb fell with a thump on Julie's very thin arm, nearly cracking the bone.

"We're strangers," said the right one, exhibiting for all the world a bit of humor. In him, wood, beard, flesh, stone and even bits of metal like those vague veins of copper in certain stones, mixed rather indiscriminately. "But why would this guy, Fourier, say that?"

"He was a Socialist," Julie explained, "He believed that insufficiently loved people, like politicians, young people on the way up, middle-management people and the plain disgusting, ought to share in the erotic wealth of the community."

"You some kind of intellectual?" said the petrified forest.

And now Julie did something very strange, which only she can do. She looked straight into his beard and made herself soft and desirable like a siren and she was almost impossibly hard to look at. She oozed the substance of the night and the air became palpable and wet, and she said, "Wittgenstein attacks diseased questions with healthy questions. We usually *know*, you see, but when we ask what it is that we know, we don't know anymore. An education based on asking questions about things we already know is not an education . . . it is a slow unravelling of the mind. *Comprende?*"

Lost in her, he had no choice. He said, "You're probably one of those types that sits up at night asking 'What is time?' " he feebly insisted.

"Time is a magazine," said Julie, pulling her arm.

"And what do you do?" said the right, to whom I "belonged." "Keep her in ears?"

I liked that. I laughed. Keeping Julie "in ears." What a delicious image. I saw her standing as a steady stream of attentively perked ears passed by her like small animals at Christmas at the SPCA. Eventually, Julie needs more and more ears to satisfy her voracious appetite for intelligent listening. I transform my body with the aid of surgery into an immense Ear, a human-sized Ear. But one day I meet the Nose, and we leave Julie and Gogol behind . . .

"I go to acupuncture class. I watch."

"I watch too," quoth he, "I watch the wires. Something comes through, I rip it and redo it in my unique style."

"Men are machines," I say.

"Love machines," he quips.

I like him. I take out my Camel Lights and start shaking them. The finely bearded wire man looks at my hand, puzzled. I look too. Instead of Camels, I'm tapping my diaphragm case. I probably blush, but I brave the sea.

"It has the yin-yang sign on it," I explain, proffering it. He recoils slightly from it, as if it were a snake. I regain my cool, and go on: "It's the first, actually, in a series of designer diaphragms I'm working on. Another says 'Will you still love me in the morning?' Stuff like that, you know." I snap it open and then shut like a cigarette case. Slip it back in my pocket. Find, pull out and light a Camel.

Julie explains to "her" bimbo: "Absolute process is absolute terror. What exactly is my interest in you? Your self? I doubt it. A life, anybody's, is a literary form to be used in the same way as a sonnet. You know, fourteen lines and *bam!*"

"I tell you one thing about reading," says the hapless, petrified gent, losing some of the silky sheen, still hoping for approval, "it doesn't help you get around in the dark . . ."

I can see that we are working apart, that soon there will be a rift, then a canyon, then a river will rush through it, and Julie and I will be standing on opposite shores, she with an enemy, me with something lukewarm like a glass of milk, and probably not too unpleasant either. I try to cross over while the crack is still only imaginary, but my burro trips and falls in.

"Julie," I speak, "I'll cast myself in an ancient myth and scare the pants off of both of them!"

"Not for my sake, I hope," the tart replies tartly. She is a language fiend, capable of swallowing a mass, a room full of people, a Third World country between the gaping words. "I don't hear you anymore," she says. "This limp, nerveless batch of new, bearded, yes-men makes me puke." She gulps down her drink, exits.

"Man," says the left, "how many shrinks does it take to change *her* lightbulb?"

"You're a growth," I tell him, and nudge his friend. But his friend doesn't laugh. "Screw you both," I declaim.

When I shove off, I notice the petrified and coppery arm of my beau trying to lift itself and fly to me and rest like a heavy bird on my shoulder. But it picks up a glass instead, and turns to the now completely still left.

Julie is nowhere to be seen, the street is full of commerce. The newsstand sells dirty magazines. The joint dealer on the corner does the boogey to internal rhythm. A dog regards a ruined Cuban sandwich. A PR gigolo I'd noticed before licks his lips as I pass. Back at the window, I call Julie. No answer. The gigolo looks up. I light a Camel. I look up.

A certain shackled limpidity is in his eyes next morning, like a flower on a window sill. The day is full of clouds and through the open window pours street jazz.

The Babysitter

MY HUSBAND was home in one of those rare weekend visits from his teaching job two states away. "We need the money," etc. Which is true, we always need *the* or money, in general, but going away is as important to him as food is to all of us. So *money* is one of those euphemisms for separation and silence, and it is a symbol as well for being "grown up," "that's how the world does it," etc. These notions are important to Mark. He would like to be perceived as a "man-in-the-world" (and when I'm not around, as a "man-of-the-world"), something solid, substantial, a "cube." He wants to (and sometimes does) project matter, thingness, substance, a thing light does not go through. He wears black or brown wingtips, baggy creased pants, nearly square ties, shirts with much collar. He quotes the classics, writes poems to Virgil ("O, Virgil, your children have taken to the streets!") and has a job translating Racine for a scholarly house, in iambic pentameter. (Well, not a "job," really. The advance was $250.00.

Instead of our usual fight, which always ended with our

daughter banging her head on the piano and calling for Peter Pan, we decided to have people over for dinner. Mark's weekend visits didn't allow for much social life together, as you may imagine. Our fights took up all our time. "Having people for dinner," was something Mark took seriously, because "that's how people do it." I was reading it more in some who's-afraid-of-virginia-woolf-sense, literally having them for dinner. Instead of pasta and white wine.

The unfortunates we chose were chosen in character-istically tactical fashion. One couple, with child (this way, the "child" would "play with" Becky) was new in town. The man was a Big Writer, a Visiting Professor in Fiction at the University. His wife was his wife. The Big Writer was from California and he was visibly wilting here on the East Coast. The wife was not known to have strong feel-ings, although it was generally assumed that she too was "wilting."

The other couple were our friends, the Alexanders. Alexander the Man, was a poet and local firebrand who would think nothing of dipping his pen in venom to attack anything that appeared to have just insulted his sense of beauty and disorder. Fairly famous, he was continually sabotaging what would have, in time, become an awesome reputation, by biting all the hands that fed him, without exception. He could also be loyal and embarassingly affec-tionate at times. He was the very opposite of the kind of Jew Mark was. Mark was the totally gentilized Jew who wished to appear Southern and Republican. Alexander was the violent partisan of whatever ideas he was wearing at the time.

The female Alexander was an artist. Quiet but shrewd, she gave things a thorough Midwestern look that approved if the thing looked or was sincere, "honest," "made of wood," "sterling," "brassy," "real." In her eyes, Mark ap-peared as the scarecrow he really is, and few others passed the test, though I think she had a certain affection for me.

It was a dinner made in the more ironic reaches of heaven, where the planners have real fun. I objected in vain. Mark thought that the prose writer and poet should meet, and that the "children should play." This is the kind of logic the Chinese erected around their Empire in order to keep the Mongolian orgies out of sight. Eventually, I was amused by the idea of the mix, and decided to keep observing as much as my role of hostess would allow. And to keep filling glasses.

BW was thin, cocained, tan, nervous. The BW Wife was anorexic, longhaired, suffering, creased downward, harried and ironic.

But their Babysitter, who hadn't been invited, was the real surprise. She was pleasingly teen-plump, chestnut haired, blue eyes, all California. She paid absolutely no attention to Baby, who was only five months old and a mix of unchanged diaper and a ready howl.

"Just give her some scraps," BW said. "In California we always bring extra people."

"That's because we only eat salad there," said the Wife.

I showed them around the living room, called Becky in to show her Baby (she turned her nose up in instant disgust, ran into her room and slammed the door through which vague TV sounds could be heard for the rest of the evening), and went to the kitchen to tend to the pasta sauce.

I heard Mark say that the Alexanders, who were due any minute, had been living for years solely on the proceeds of his published literary works, without teaching. BW, whose literary earnings must have been eighty times the size of Alexander's, said thinly: "Big deal!" In addition to those earnings, BW had a fat university job in California, and moved around the country and abroad, exchanging semesters with other professors.

"He's got another wife to support," observed the Wife apropos her hubby, "and another set of kids, both of whom are junkies."

"I don't think Myron is a junkie," the Babysitter said firmly. "He fires but he's not hooked."

"He's a weekend junkie," agreed BW.

This was already more than our little world could safely take. Mark changed the tack, as tactfully as he could, which can be brutal.

"Translating high classical French," he said, "can be extremely difficult, but the rewards are great."

Usually, at this point in our provinces, someone calls for a recitation and Mark is only too happy to oblige. He reads in a stentorian voice, picked up from God knows what old record, maybe from the first poetry reading ever, Lord Alfred Tennyson reading "The Charge of The Light Brigade."

But the Wife said, "Bullshit. Anybody who's been firing as long as that is a fucking junkie. If he couldn't get it for a week, he'd turn into a snivelling little worm, begging for what's left in a whore's cruddy cooker!" The pasta sauce was bubbling and I swear I saw a thin-lipped smile in the tomato red. It was like the triumph of language over pasta, or the "Comeback of the Wife" or something. In any case, something glorious and exhausting. Mark, I knew, was speechless.

But just as calmly as if that had been only a normal quip in the course of the many sets of quips that hold our social lives in shape, BW said, "I don't suppose you mean to point out our similarities with that metaphor? Like father like son, and all that. Sort of like, 'The son will lick the crud in the whore's spoon, while the father will go for the rest of the whore.' Very good, dear. Excellent."

Echoed by the Babysitter: "Just as you said in your book, LANGUAGE AND MANNERS, page 28, 'second-strike language can devastate *leisurely*. . . .'"

Which is when the front door started banging furiously. Alexander didn't believe in doors. He thought they should be knocked down. I came to let them in. Passing on my way through the living room, everyone looked peaceful and sunny sipping wine. Could I have hallucinated all those words? Mark was standing by the bookcase with an early edition of *Phèdre* in his hand.

Alexander kissed me hard on one cheek, and would have liked to pat my behind, I'm sure. Alexandra pecked me too and appraised me cooly, down through the tomato spots on my apron. She said: "I'll help you," and Alexander advanced right into the middle of the livingroom, zeroed in on BW, held out his hand and said: "I hear your new book's making a shitload of money!"

"I can't complain," BW said sourly.

The Wife and Baby were then introduced to the new couple, but not the Babysitter.

"Who are you, the Babysitter?" asked Alexander.

"How did you know?" said the Wife.

"Blue eyes, pug nose, adoring smile," said Alexander. "We used to live in California."

At this point, Alexandra and I went into the kitchen, and I took out the plates, and she broke the spaghetti box and dropped the noodles in the boiling water.

Alexander's vehement voice said: "How much did you make?"

I couldn't hear the answer, because Alexandra said, "They brought a babysitter all the way from the *West Coast?*"

BW's new book was called THE BOYS' ROOM, and it was being touted as the season's hottest property. In reality, the hype had to do with the success of the earlier THE WOMEN'S ROOM, by Marilyn French. It was commonplace in publishing circles that the first man to write a similar roll of toilet paper, would make a wad. And now here it was, THE BOYS' ROOM, the story of four or five guys getting drunk and spilling all the male-chauvinist-pig beans that had been simmering in them for years, ever since women's lib had been going around with razor blades looking for balls.

"Dinner is on," I said, advancing two steps into the

room. Everyone came in, except the Babysitter.

"I put out a plate and a chair for her," I said. "There is plenty for everybody."

"I will take her plate to her," said BW. "She's the Baby-sitter." The Baby, last I'd seen him, had curled up in a corner with Becky's large felt monkey, and had gone to sleep in a puddle of feces and urine.

My protest went unheeded, and BW filled a plate heaping full of pasta, poured a lot of sauce on it, and went into the other room. There was a fork planted in the top of the mound, and just as he exited, he grabbed a *second* fork.

"Now what do you suppose that *second* fork is for?" asked the wife.

Mark refilled the glasses with wine, and we sat down to eat. Passing the parmesan, rolling up the noodles, swishing the wine and getting ready for that first bite, took a little time. Nobody said anything.

"Good food," said Mark to me, the first words he had directed my way since coming home for the weekend. "I miss home cooking," he said to everyone else.

"We eat out," said the BW Wife. "BW eats out too."

"I could review THE BOYS' ROOM, for the underground paper," said Alexander, "if he gives me a copy."

"*The New York Times* will review it on the front page," came BW's voice from the other room, "as will all the other big places. But I would be very interested in what a place like *that* would have to say!"

Now he'd done it. Alexander put his fork down slowly, and said to the invisible BW: "A place like *what?*"

There was a giggle in the living room, coming from the Babysitter, and BW, his mouth full of pasta, said chewing: "Underground, those kinds of people. . . ."

"And who the fuck are those *kinds?* Do they matter less than the riffraff who read the bourgeois sheets?"

There was more giggling, and then the Babysitter said, "That's not what he meant. On page 78 of LANGUAGE there is a quote from Walter Benjamin . . ."

"Why doesn't he come in here?" said Alexandra.

"He's feeding the Babysitter," the wife said.

Good hostess that I am, I said: "Lets have a toast for THE BOYS' ROOM, may it prosper!" Everyone raised their glasses, and clinked, except for Alexander who made a point of drawing out and then sucking in a very long noodle.

"Chin chin," said BW from the living room, and there was a clink of glasses out there.

After that, we ate quietly. Alexandra noted the pretty mugs for coffee, and she said that you could get a similar red wine cheaper at Frank's. The wife closed up like a shell, opening up only to suck in noodles. Mark brought Racine up two more times but dropped him for lack of interest. Alexander puffed a few times as if he were going to say something, but disgust soon showed on his face and he tended to his food. Occasional giggling came from the other room.

Afterwards, everyone took their coffee back into the living room. BW was sitting in the rocking chair with his eyes half-closed, rocking a little. The Babysitter was changing the baby from an oversized box of Pampers I hadn't noticed before. The soiled diaper lay next to her like a flag captured in battle.

"I think he's sleepy," she said to the wife. "Maybe I should take him home."

"Let *her* take him home," said BW, meaning the wife.

"I will," she said, and caught deftly the car keys BW threw suddenly at her.

"OK," said the Babysitter, "I'll see that BW gets home safely," and she took out a stick of gum.

The Alexanders left soon after the wife did. Mark tried to make some kind of conversation, but BW and the Babysitter started making out on the floor, next to the diaper no one had bothered to throw out. There seemed to be some kind of invitation for us to join in their petting. Some kind of California manners, no doubt. But Mark and I don't do that kind of thing. I went in to put Becky to bed, and Mark went to his office to read or pretend to read.

When we left the room, BW and Babysitter turned off the light.

A Bar in Brooklyn

MY SEARCH for anonymity took me all the way to Brooklyn. I saw a Happy Hour sign in the window of a teeming watering hole and went in. I took the only stool in the sea of suits and imagined myself to be a slim sloop maneuvering the straits between the bulky tankers in the Gulf of Aqaba. A bubbling office siren to my right was emptying the contents of a coconut shell into her hold through a pink straw. But at my left — I had to do a double take. At my left was a priest.

His left hand, next to me, was planted on the bar at the elbow and a smoking cigarette bloomed from its fingers. Next to his other hand, which lay limply and ecclesiastically (as in "a holy hand") on the bar, was a Manhattan in a tall glass. The cigarette hand had a ring on the matrimonial finger. His fingernails were rosy and well clipped.

I ordered another (it was two drinks for the price of one) in order to steel myself for conversation with the man of the cloth. But as I involved myself in ordering, another floozie, born no doubt from the ground oyster shells that littered the floor of the establishment, took the father on. I say another floozie because when I search for anonymity *I'm* a floozie. She was a chestnut-haired, ruby-lipsticked nymph with a bottle of Bud in her hand. The business suit gave in to all kind of topography.

"Taking refuge from the sanctuary?" was what I had planned to ask him.

"Seeking asylum from the eternal verities?" was what she asked him.

That wasn't bad. And then she said: "I don't mean to impose," And that *was* bad. Quite plainly, she was imposing.

The priest was young. Forty at most, blond, pale, handsome and sensual, if not downright corrupt around the mouth.

"Not at all," he said. "The thing is, God is fairly indulgent. He's forgiven people for more than a Manhattan."

"And cigarettes?" the floozie asked.

It's exactly what *I* would have said. Maybe floozies are generic. I looked a little closer at my competition. Her sneer reminded me of one similar in a pic of myself, taken at Ocean City, Maryland, when I was fifteen and had just lost my cherry.

"That's a sin, I admit," the father said sadly. "Tried to kick it several times but every time it gains on me again. I wake up at night and see a little glowing tip inches from my face, tempting me." He half-closed his pale, weary lids in the likeness of a suffering man.

"The fathers of the desert should've had it so hard," laughed the hussy.

Father opened one eye, then the other, and switched gears. His voice took on the upper edge of the pulpit basso. "And you? Have you no vices, friend? Are you not stereotyping me in your mind, right now, quicker than I can dissuade you?"

"I try not to," she said, allowing a kind of velveteen chill into her voice. I felt it, and people must have felt it three stools away, because there was suddenly that silent bubble in the place, that sometimes opens abruptly in a noisy room and everybody can hear clearly the last thing said. Everybody looked at the priest, and then at the girl, and the understanding that surpasses all knowing gripped everyone, and then the noise resumed.

I was most intrigued by her at this point. I took her proportions mentally, using my palms to measure her in my mind from her moderately high high-heels to the part in her hair. She was about my height, and built similarly if one allowed for exaggerations and costume differences. It was a little spooky, and I decided to play avant-echo, to see if we did resemble each other all that much. I decided to say quickly to myself whatever seemed appropriate, before she made her replies.

The father, embarrassed by the silence but now relieved by the noise, and on his second Manhattan as well, said, "Any man's reputation can be ruined here, leave alone that of a servant of the Lord."

"Let's get back to your sins," I said to myself.

"We left off at the glowing tip," said she.

"Now, now," teased the priest, "Let's not get carried away. I'm a man, I have feelings."

"What kind of feelings?"

"What kind of feelings?"

I shifted uncomfortably. I said: "Jinx. You owe me a Coke."

"What?" said the floozie.

"Nothing," I mumbled. "Just thinking."

"Seriously though," she said to him. "Don't you find any contradiction between this bar and your duties?"

That was quick, I hadn't had time to get in an avant-echo.

"Not to delve too deeply, dear, but God is bigger than His contradictions. He really does forgive. He may in fact preside equally over picket-fences and tanks, over His Left and His Right, if the truth were known."

"Thanks," I said, because I was his left.

"I'm Episcopalian," he continued, "but in the Catholic Church God is divided between the rich and the poor, and between men and women. The clergy, the theologians, the wealthy prefer Jesus, while the poor and women and most of South America worship the Virgin of Perpetual Sorrow. The strong wield theology like a nightstick, the poor yield their tears like little bombs of grief. In any case, it's bound to end badly."

The father stopped short. Emotion had crept into his voice about halfway through this speech, and he'd surprised himself. I don't think he meant to say all that. He flushed and a number of freckles appeared like a strange constellation beneath the pale skin.

"That's some kind of revolutionary Manichaeism," I said to myself.

"You sound like a leftwing Nicaraguan," said she.

Now that was definitely out of her league. She just wasn't dressed the part for those words. Where would a lipsticked bimbo working in an office in Lower Slobovia get that kind of quick grasp? I looked closely at her, and as I looked I thought that I discerned dark lines under her eyes, barely covered by makeup. Her hands were shaking a little too, and on the wrist of one of them, just under the flowered sleeve of her blouse was a black mark. It could have been a speck of dirt or it could have been the outermost edge of a tattoo that began on one of her breasts and went down her arm to end just below the sleeve.

"And I didn't mean to upset you," she was saying.

Her bluster turned quickly into an apology. I was beginning to lose interest, and was just turning toward my right where, for the past few moments I had become aware of a massive bulk of horny meat, when I saw the father reach under his tunic.

From under there he extracted a Pelikan fountainpen. He took off the top and the gold nib glinted for a moment in the light refracted through my whiskey. He pulled the half-soggy napkin between us quickly toward him and scribbled a few words in rapid cursive. He handed it to her. She put it in her skirt pocket without reading it, and held the priest's gaze in her own. Between them, ionized particles and magnetized atoms rushed to form an intense field. It was blinding. My heart fluttered like a dove.

"OK, then," I said to myself, but she said nothing.